Seventh-Grade

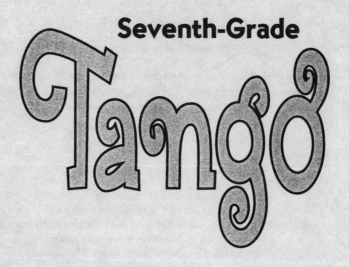

Tango

ELIZABETH LEVY

Hyperion Paperbacks for Children • New York

Copyright © 2000 by Elizabeth Levy
For information address Hyperion Paperbacks for Children, 114 Fifth Avenue,
New York, New York 10011-5690.
First paperback edition, 2001
1 3 5 7 9 10 8 6 4 2
Library of Congress Cataloguing-in-Publication Data
Levy, Elizabeth.
Seventh-grade tango / Elizabeth Levy. — 1st ed.
p. cm.
Summary: When Rebecca, a seventh-grader, is paired up with her friend Scott for a dance class at school, she learns a lot about who her real friends are.
ISBN 0-7868-0498-X (trade) — ISBN 0-7868-2427-1 (lib. ed.) — ISBN 0-7868-1565-5 (pbk.)
[1. Dancers—Fiction. 2. Friendship—Fiction. 3. Schools—Fiction.] I. Title.
PZ7.L587 SE 2000
[Fic—dc21   99-53124

Visit www.hyperionchildrensbooks.com

To Paul Lester,
who teaches us to dance from the core
and from the heart

Contents

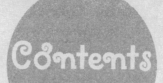

1

Hey There, Killer Dancer

The night Scott gave Rebecca the nickname "Killer Dancer" had started out great. At their graduation dance from sixth grade, Scott and Rebecca were doing a fast dance together. Out on the dance floor, they felt fabulous. When one spun, the other spun, too. When one jumped, the other jumped just as high. Their eyes kept meeting as they picked up each other's slightest cues and rhythms— a quick cut to the left—a cut to the right.

Then Rebecca took one spin too fast. She spun into the food table and knocked over the punch bowl. She tried to right the punch bowl, but slipped on the wet floor, and three dozen pizzas slid off the table. Nobody could believe that one spin could do so much damage. Scott helped her, but it took about a half hour to get the gooey cheese off the dance floor.

After the pizza fiasco, Rebecca was a nervous

wreck. Even under normal times Rebecca had a lot of energy, but now she was wired so tight that anything could happen—and it did. They were doing the hokeypokey—a dance that even as a sixth grader Rebecca knew was childish. Rebecca had been wearing platform shoes that she had never worn before. She had always been tall for her age, and in sixth grade she had suddenly sprouted up another three inches. In her platform shoes, she was five feet eight. She put her left foot in, but when she swung her left foot to "put it out," her platform heel smashed on Scott's toe—hard. He screamed. By the time Scott took off his shoe and sock, his second toe had already started to turn purple. Scott looked up at her in amazement and said, "Rebecca, you really are a killer dancer."

That had been the last day of school. Rebecca sent Scott a get-well card to his camp, but she hadn't seen or heard from Scott all summer. The first morning of seventh grade, Scott greeted Rebecca by shouting, "Hey, K.D."

"K.D.?" repeated Rebecca, although she knew perfectly well what the initials stood for. Scott had grown over the summer. He was now almost as tall as Rebecca. He was still skinny, but his limbs had more muscle on them. Scott's face was different from those of most boys that Rebecca knew—every emotion showed on it. When he was bored, it showed. When he was excited, that showed, too. He now looked excited to see Rebecca, and that made her fidgety.

"How's your toe?" Rebecca asked him. Boys' voices are supposed to crack at thirteen—not girls' voices. But Rebecca's voice reached a high squeak on the word "toe." Scott looked at her oddly.

"My toe's fine now. But the first month of camp, I couldn't play the drums. Nobody ever thinks of it—but you need your feet to play the drums. So how was your summer? You break any other people's toes?"

"No, Scott. Believe it or not, the toes around me were safe all summer."

"I guess you must not have danced much," teased Scott.

"I was at basketball camp," replied Rebecca dryly.

"Cool," said Scott. Rebecca was glad he thought that was cool. The truth was that it had been a shock to her system to find out how many girls were better basketball players than she was. In elementary school, Rebecca had been one of the best. Her father was convinced she would win a basketball scholarship to college. Now Rebecca wasn't so sure. She knew she didn't love basketball with the same passion that Scott felt for the drums.

"I meant to write you from camp," said Scott. "I wanted to tell you thanks for my get-well card." He continued in a sing-song voice, "*Oh woe, oh no, I feel so low/I wish I had never broken your toe/I hope you will not be my foe. . . .*"

Rebecca felt herself blush. She couldn't believe that he had memorized it.

"I'll see you, K.D.," said Scott.

"Rebecca, the name is *Rebecca*!" shouted Rebecca after him. Rebecca loved her name. She was named after her great-grandmother on her father's side. Her father had given Rebecca a faded photo of the original Rebecca. She was sitting in the driver's seat of one of the very first Model T automobiles, wearing a white hat that tied under her chin.

"You were named after a remarkable woman," said Rebecca's father when he gave her the photo. "Automobiles were so new when my grandmother bought one that she didn't know it went backward. If she wanted to get somewhere, she just kept going forward. When she found out that the car had a gear for going backward, she said she didn't like it—and refused to ever drive in reverse." Rebecca's father had laughed when he told her the story, but it was clear to Rebecca that her father admired the woman who had refused to go backward.

Rebecca *had* been going backward when she stepped on Scott's toe, so maybe there was a lesson in that. Maybe if she hadn't gone backward she wouldn't have to live with the nickname Killer Dancer. Within days, it was apparent that Killer Dancer was the name Rebecca was going to be stuck with. It spread around the school like wildfire. By the second week of school, even kids who had never met Rebecca before were calling her "K.D."

One of them was Adrienne, a girl who had just transferred to their school. She was almost as tall as Rebecca, which made them two of the tallest girls in the class. Rebecca liked that there was someone new who was almost as tall as she was. It made her feel less awkward.

"Why do people call you Killer Dancer?" asked Adrienne. "Are you really that great a dancer? Show me your moves."

Rebecca laughed. "Believe me, my dance moves are nothing to write home about."

"That's not what I hear."

"Rebecca *is* a good dancer," said Samantha, one of Rebecca's friends. About three inches shorter than Rebecca, Samantha was the kind of girl for whom the adjective "cute" was created. Boys especially found her cute, and she loved having boyfriends. Yet the fact that she adored boys didn't mean that she turned into a puddle in front of them. Rebecca was more than a little in awe of Samantha's fearlessness with boys.

"It's not Rebecca's fault she broke Scott's toe," said Samantha. Just the way she said it made Rebecca feel guilty all over again.

"You broke a guy's toe?" asked Adrienne incredulously. Rebecca explained about the hokeypokey.

"That should teach you not to do the hokeypokey," said Adrienne.

"Now you know the story of why Scott calls her Killer Dancer," explained Samantha. "Everybody else picked it up from him."

"Let's not keep repeating it," said Rebecca hopefully. "Maybe it'll die off."

Perhaps the nickname *would* have died off. Nicknames tend to change quickly in middle school. However, it was Rebecca's fate that the nickname Killer Dancer was about to take on a whole new meaning.

2

The Day Ballroom Dancing Invaded Middle School

The day that ballroom dancing invaded school came with no warning in October. Every Friday morning the William T. Harris Middle School had an assembly on what were called the "core virtues." Students were asked to stand and pledge to strengthen the virtues of trustworthiness, kindness, caring, courtesy, hard work, respect, responsibility, self-control, honesty, and fairness.

On this particular Friday morning assembly, Rebecca ended up in a row next to Scott. It wasn't easy to give a pledge to be kind, caring, and courteous, standing next to someone whose limb you had already broken—even if was just a tiny limb. After all, it was his second toe, not his big toe.

"Good morning, girls and boys," said Dr. Divinas. She tapped the mike. "Today, I have an exciting announcement. Our school has been chosen for a pilot program in the arts. All of you girls and boys

7

are going to be taught ballroom dancing twice a week for the rest of the year."

Rebecca giggled. She couldn't help herself. Maybe it was because she was sitting next to Scott and he had named her Killer Dancer. Maybe it was because the idea of dancing with a boy in school was so embarrassing. She wasn't the only one. Giggles rippled through the assembly like a tidal wave.

Dr. Divinas did not look amused. "I know that many of you are going to feel shy and embarrassed at first as you learn the social graces of dancing together."

Who knew why the words "social graces" were so funny? But they were. Rebecca caught Scott's eye and he was snickering, too. Rebecca gave out one of those snorts that start in your nose and then kind of shudder through you. Apparently it was catching. Soon their entire row sounded like a series of firecrackers. *Snort-giggle-snort-giggle.*

"Girls and boys!" shouted Dr. Divinas in a voice that told them they were in trouble. "The giddiness will end here! Now!"

Rebecca tried to straighten up and hold in her snorts.

Dr. Divinas continued. "As I'm sure many of you know, ballroom dancing is now an Olympic exhibition sport. By the year 2008, it will be an official sport. However, we are not just introducing ballroom dancing as a sport. I applied for this grant because I believe that it fits into our program of Building a Culture of Character. In addition to learning to dance, I expect you to learn manners. You will learn how to treat members of the opposite sex courteously and how to work together as partners with someone of the opposite sex." Dr. Divinas paused as if daring them to snicker at the fact that their very own principal had used the word "sex" twice in a sentence.

Dr. Divinas went on. "In your dance lessons, you will have an opportunity to apply many of our core virtues—courtesy, kindness, hard work, respect, and self-control."

"Only Divinas could make dance into something that sounds like it comes from military school," muttered Scott.

"Being funny is not on Divinas's list of core virtues," Rebecca whispered back. Scott grinned at Rebecca. It surprised Rebecca how much it pleased her.

"Now, girls and boys, give a warm welcome to your dance teacher, Mr. Bruce DePalma from the Dance America Center."

The teacher had dark hair and he looked more like a swimmer than a dancer—his torso was long and muscled. He smiled out at the audience. It was obvious that he was a man who was used to being looked at, but he still radiated real warmth.

"Good morning, girls and boys." He had a voice that seemed to come from deep inside him. He told them that they would be learning five dances: the merengue, fox-trot, waltz, tango, and swing. At the end of the year in May, the top dancing team from the school would be entered in a citywide competition in which Broadway and Hollywood choreographers would be the judges.

"I was fascinated by your list of core virtues," he said. He bowed to Dr. Divinas, and then he held his hand out to her. She took it. He twirled her toward him and then sent her spinning out. They did a series of jitterbug steps. He swept her back into his arms and they circled the stage. Dr. Divinas had a huge smile on her face. She suddenly looked youthful. Mr. DePalma stopped and bowed to her.

Then he went forward to the microphone. "Girls and boys," he said, not even winded. "I wonder if you can think of one core that wasn't mentioned."

"Fun!" Rebecca shouted. She felt 100 percent confident "fun" was the word he was looking for. The gorgeous dance teacher smiled at Rebecca. Rebecca beamed her delight at him, feeling as if they were sharing a private moment.

"Fun is a great answer," he said. "But in a way, the fun is almost a by-product. It wasn't the answer I was looking for."

Scott glanced at Rebecca. He could see she felt crushed. Rebecca didn't see Scott's pitying glance, though. Her eyes were focused solely on the dance teacher. He smiled out at the audience, but to Rebecca, his eyes seemed to be searching her out.

"The reason why your talk about core virtues fascinated me," continued Mr. DePalma, "is because dancers are always talking about our core—our center. None of the core virtues matters if you don't have a core. All dance starts from our center."

He tapped himself on his stomach. His back moved and his arms went wide. He twirled around. Rebecca had seen dancers twirl before, but his twirl seemed to come from inside. Despite the movement, there was something still about it. Nothing was hurried. He did a few steps, his feet pointing first in one direction and then in the other. Rebecca was mesmerized by the way his torso moved. It was soft, and then long, and then soft again. It enchanted her the way a cobra mesmerizes its victims before it strikes.

He took a hold of the microphone. "We dance from our center, and when we dance with another person, the wonderful thing about it is that we can find the other person's center, too. When that happens, you dance together beautifully—and that kind of ballroom dancing is magical."

"And sometimes you'll almost lose a toe in the magic," Scott whispered into Rebecca's ear.

3

Can You Imagine Kissing Scott?

On the weekend before dance classes were supposed to begin, Rebecca got a cold. Normally when Rebecca was sick, she loved it when the digital thermometer beeped in her mouth like a little song, saying: Stay home, *beep*, watch TV, *beep*, don't go to school, *beep*. This time, however, Rebecca kept taking the thermometer out of her mouth before the beeps were done.

"Normal," her mom announced cheerfully.

"Yay!" shouted Rebecca, throwing off the bed-covers.

"I'm so glad that you still love school," said her mom. "I read that often girls in middle school lose their enthusiasm for school."

"Maybe more schools should have Mr. DePalma come in and teach dance," said Rebecca.

Her mother smiled. "That's your new dance teacher, right?"

Rebecca nodded.

"Well, I think you'll be able to go to school on Monday, no problem," said her mom.

Samantha called Rebecca at home to see how she felt. "Mom says that if I still don't have a fever, I can go to school on Monday," Rebecca said. "I would have died if I had to miss our first dance class."

"I know what you mean," said Samantha. "That dance teacher is cuter than cute. Everybody is talking about it. He is such a hunk."

Rebecca didn't want everyone else to think that Mr. DePalma was cuter than cute or a hunk. She wanted to be the only one who saw how beautiful he was. She sneezed into the phone.

"*Ew!* Are you okay?" Samantha asked.

"No, I'm not," said Rebecca. "My nose is red. I look like Rudolph, the Red-Nosed Reindeer and sound like Porky the Pig. My ears are stuffed. I can't hear. Nobody is going to want to dance with me. I'll probably miss a beat and kill somebody for real this time."

"Nonsense," said Samantha. "Think of these dance classes as a chance for a clean slate. Scott Lee's broken toe is history. It's time you got a real boyfriend—someone like Shane."

Rebecca was glad that Samantha couldn't see the face she was making at the mention of Shane. Shane was an eighth grader with a face that looked like a pizza. He had somehow managed to grow a little goatee on his chin of spiky little red tufts. Shane had also perfected the art of making rude noises out of his armpit. Personally, Rebecca did not believe a goatee, pimples, and the ability to make your armpit sound like your butt added up to cuter than cute. However, she had learned that there was simply no accounting for who Samantha would find attractive.

"Shane is definitely *one* of my boyfriends," confirmed Samantha. "I like that Shane is older. But he said that he didn't want to have just one girlfriend— so I can have more than one boyfriend."

Rebecca sighed. Here Samantha was, talking about having more than one boyfriend. Rebecca had never really had one—except for in third grade—and that had practically been a joke. One day at a neighborhood picnic, Scott and Rebecca decided to tell everybody they were girlfriend and boyfriend. They went on a "date" to go get ice cream. The date lasted exactly fifteen minutes. Then they both declared to their families that they were bored and were breaking up.

What nobody knew was that before they had gotten bored, Rebecca and Scott had gone behind the ice cream truck and danced. They had danced holding each other to the little jingle of the truck. When the dance was over, they tried out a kiss. Third graders' kisses are supposed to be yucky—but theirs wasn't. It lasted less than seven seconds, but neither Rebecca nor Scott had forgotten about it. Yet they never talked about it, either.

"Do you think Scott will ever dance with me?" wondered Rebecca. "After I broke his toe . . ."

Samantha ignored the question. "I bet Shane's a cool dancer. We'll look cute dancing together in class."

"He probably keeps the rhythm by flapping his armpit in the air," replied Rebecca.

"Don't make fun of people who happen to be more mature than you are," said Samantha.

"Shane—*mature*?" repeated Rebecca. "Please don't tell me that playing 'The Star-Spangled Banner' from your armpit is a sign of maturity. Give me one example of Shane being mature."

"Well," said Samantha, taking her time to answer, "Shane believes that we are incredibly immature because we have parties where we don't play kissing games."

"That's an example of maturity?"

"We're in seventh grade. We should have been playing long ago."

"Maybe we can enroll in Remedial Kissing 101," said Rebecca. "I'd take that course if Mr. DePalma was teaching it." She giggled.

"Stop giggling about it. Kissing Mr. DePalma is just a fantasy. I told you—it's time you thought about getting a boyfriend. And having real kisses."

Rebecca licked her lips. The truth was humiliating. She would be thirteen in February. Except for Scott and that dance that ended with a kiss behind the ice cream truck, she had never really kissed a boy. She wished they *did* have a course on remedial kissing.

"How about Scott?" asked Rebecca. "He and I have been friends forever. Maybe he'll let me practice kissing with him."

"Scott would *not* be a good boyfriend for you, Rebecca," said Samantha. No one could accuse Samantha of not having definite opinions. "You've known each other too long. You're too good friends."

"What's wrong with having a friend for a boyfriend?" asked Rebecca.

"Pu-leeze," said Samantha. "I mean, can you imagine kissing Scott?"

Rebecca could. Quite easily. She could even remember what it had been like. She wondered what it would be like to kiss him now.

Four Feet Pretending to Be Two

On Monday morning the class lined up to go into the gym for the first dance class. Everyone was jostling each other and giggling. Rebecca could barely crack a smile, but not because she was depressed. Far from it. She was focused, like an athlete before a big game. She felt separate from everyone else, excited, as if she were going on a grand adventure that was just for her.

Bruce DePalma was wearing a Hawaiian shirt and loose pants. It was as if a tropical flower had suddenly landed at the Harris School. Rebecca couldn't think of one teacher whom she had ever seen in a Hawaiian shirt.

He was standing in the middle of the gym, fiddling with the controls of the CD player. He was playing Latin music and doing salsa steps by himself. Rebecca knew that she was not supposed to stare at a teacher's hips. In fact, it was almost an unwritten rule that you were not supposed to even notice that teachers have hips. But Mr. DePalma had hips, and he moved them so effortlessly that it was like water playing in a stream.

In the midst of staring at him, Rebecca sneezed. It was a wet sneeze that came out so quickly she couldn't catch all the snot in her hand. Mr. DePalma stopped dancing and turned to her. "God bless you."

He fished a tissue out of his pocket and handed it to her. Rebecca wiped her hand. He smiled at her. "Why don't you go wash your hands? In dance class, we touch each other—and you don't want to be spreading germs."

"Yeah, well she's already known as K.D.," said Shane. Rebecca shot Shane a dirty look, and she was glad to see that Samantha had poked Shane with her elbow and whispered to him to *shut up*.

"I'm just getting over a cold," Rebecca told Mr. DePalma.

"The doctor said there was no reason she couldn't come to school," chirped up Samantha.

Mr. DePalma smiled. "If the doctor said you could come to school, I'm sure you can dance. Personally, I believe that dance is the cure for the common cold."

Rebecca went to the bathroom and washed her

hands. She looked at herself in the mirror. Her nose still looked red. She scrubbed her hands hard, wanting to be sure that she didn't infect Mr. DePalma with cooties.

She went back out to the gym. "All right, girls and boys," said Mr. DePalma. "Gather in a big circle around me. Space yourself out—girl-boy, girl-boy. Don't worry who you're standing next to. For the first several classes, we'll be changing partners. We'll rotate every few minutes."

Everybody stood frozen like statues. Apparently Mr. DePalma knew nothing about the behavior of seventh and eighth graders. Girls never officially stood next to the boys if it could be avoided. The teachers had long since resigned themselves to having girls in one line and boys in the other, just to avoid the pushing and shoving. It was as if nobody knew how to do what Mr. DePalma wanted.

"Come on! Move it!" Mr. DePalma suddenly shouted. He had a different shout than most teachers. It was loud, but it sounded friendly, the way a coach on a sitcom might sound. The real miracle was that the class did exactly what he asked. Just like that. They quickly lined up in a circle, girl-boy, girl-boy. Rebecca ended up standing between Daniel Williams and Shane. Daniel was almost a head shorter than

Rebecca. He was undergoing his second round of braces to correct an overbite. He had big teeth, and they looked even bigger with the metal on them. Daniel considered himself the put-down king. He didn't even realize that at least in Rebecca's eyes, being the put-down king was the biggest insult of them all.

"All right," said Mr. DePalma. "Girls, when you come into this room, you need to forget all your leadership qualities that are so important. I know you're being raised to be President, and the bosses of your company. That's terrific. But here, you've got to follow. Some of you may have heard of Fred Astaire and Ginger Rogers. Later in the semester I'll bring in some videos to show you. Fred Astaire is considered the best dancer of all time—even star ballet dancers think that he's the tops. But, someone once said that Ginger Rogers was the real hero. Because she had to do all the steps Fred did—only backward and in high heels.

"Now, boys—just because you're the leaders— this does not mean that you can shove your partner around. You have to watch out for her at all times. She's your responsibility. She trusts you. You've got to be looking out to see where the other couples are. You're the one who's got to give her the clues. This isn't easy."

This was already sounding impossible. He was crazy—asking a seventh- or eighth-grade girl to follow a boy, going backward—asking girls and boys to trust each other! Mr. DePalma stood in the center of the circle. He kept turning to take them all in. "Girls, face the boy to your left and put your left hand on his right shoulder," he ordered.

Rebecca put her hand on Daniel's shoulder. He stuck his nose in her breastbone. Rebecca pushed him away. "Take each other's free hand," instructed Mr. DePalma. "Now, step together, step sideways, step together." Every time they were supposed to step sideways, Daniel stepped in toward Rebecca, his nose landing inches from her chest bone. Rebecca pushed him back so hard that he tripped over his own feet.

"Sideways!" shouted Mr. DePalma. Rebecca and Daniel zigzagged across the floor like a mechanical windup toy gone amuck. For every sideways step, Daniel pushed forward and Rebecca pushed him back.

Thankfully, after less than a minute, Mr. DePalma told them to change partners. They kept moving around the circle.

Halfway around the circle, Scott took Rebecca's hand. They were now nearly exactly the same height.

Rebecca moved her left foot to the side, just as Scott moved his right. Step-together, step-together. They moved in unison around the circle, their hips swaying just slightly, right, left, right, left. Rebecca's hand relaxed on Scott's shoulder. Scott stopped looking at his feet and lifted his head.

Then it was time to move on to the next partner. Mr. DePalma turned off the music. "Okay, that was a good start, but now I have a riddle for you. What is four feet pretending to be two?"

Rebecca thought hard. She didn't want to blurt out an answer the way she had in assembly.

"An alien!" shouted out Shane.

Mr. DePalma shook his head, no.

The more Rebecca tried to think of an animal with four feet pretending to be two, the more she kept seeing an ostrich mating with another ostrich. She knew that wasn't right.

Scott raised his hand. Mr. DePalma called on him. "What do you think the answer is?" he asked.

"A couple dancing together. They'd have four feet pretending to be two," said Scott. His voice cracked as he answered. Rebecca turned to him. Scott's voice always sounded like he had a cold, but it rarely cracked. She wondered if he was as nervous as she was.

The class erupted into hoots and howls. Scott looked down at the ground. Rebecca could tell he felt mortified.

Mr. DePalma clapped his hands together. It was amazing the sound that he could get by bringing just two hands together. The class quieted down instantly.

"What's your name?" he asked Scott.

Scott told him.

"Very good, Scott. That was exactly the right answer. When two people dance together they *are* four feet pretending to be two. When they are really dancing together, they aren't pretending, they actually *are* four feet that are two. How many of you girls remember when you learned to dance—dancing on top of your father's shoes?"

Rebecca raised her hand slowly, so did Adrienne and Samantha and almost all the girls in the circle. Rebecca figured any mention of dancing on someone's toes would elicit a crack about her. Yet nobody said a word. Everybody was listening to Mr. DePalma without a giggle. The fact that Mr. DePalma took dance so seriously seemed to sink in. It was amazing. Even the kids like Shane and Daniel, who were the worst cutups, looked at Mr. DePalma intensely.

Rebecca *could* remember her father holding her on his shoes at weddings and parties and dancing her around the room. She had loved it. She couldn't remember when exactly she had gotten too big to do it any longer.

"How many people speak English?" asked Mr. DePalma. He changed subjects so abruptly that he kept their attention.

"Is this another riddle?" asked Shane.

Mr. DePalma shook his head. "No. Answer the question. How many of you speak English?" Everyone raised their hands slowly, even Illiana, who'd just come from Russia.

"How many speak Spanish?" asked Mr. DePalma. About half of the class raised their hands.

"How many Japanese?" he asked. Several kids taking karate raised their hands even though their Japanese was limited to counting to ten.

"Korean?" Kai and Sam Seo raised their hands.

"Hindi?"

The questions came fast and furious.

"All right," said Mr. DePalma. "*I* am fluent in a language that every one in the world speaks. In my class, you are all going to be learning this language— and yet it's one that you already know. What is it?"

"Another riddle?" asked Samantha.

Mr. DePalma smiled at her. "Yes, I love riddles." he said. "Do you know the answer?"

"Give me a minute," said Samantha. She gave him her most charming smile as if there would never be any doubt that the teacher and the entire class would be happy to wait forever for Samantha's answer. Mr. DePalma smiled back.

A new language that we already know. Rebecca wanted the answer so badly, but her mind was a blank. She wished she could get her mind off herself dancing on her father's shoes.

"Body language?" Samantha shouted out before Rebecca or anybody else could come up with an answer.

Mr. DePalma beamed at her. "Yes." Samantha gave Mr. DePalma a radiant smile.

"Body language is the way you stand and move," said Mr. DePalma. "It shows the world what you think. I need a volunteer. May I have a young woman?"

His words were startling. Other teachers used the words "young woman," and it sounded like a reprimand. From Mr. DePalma, the words "young woman" sounded like an invitation to join his world. Just hearing the word "woman" come from Mr. DePalma's lips made Rebecca's insides do flips. He

26

was looking for a young woman and she could be the one.

Across the circle, Samantha's hand shot up. When Samantha's hand went up, her eyes sparkled and teachers called on her. It was not a goody-goody thing. Teacher's eyes always went right to Samantha.

Rebecca didn't even realize that her hand had gone up, too. It was almost as if it had a will of its own. Without saying a word, Mr. DePalma walked over to Rebecca and looked into her eyes. He held out his hands with his palm up in front of her. He smiled and gave a slight bow.

For a split second, Rebecca wondered if he wanted to see if she had really washed her hands. She looked at his hands and then into his eyes. She knew he wanted her to put her hands in his. She did. His hands felt callused and strong and dry.

He led her out into the center of the circle. Rebecca looked down on the floor. Mr. DePalma gestured with his palm for her to lift her chin. It was the first time she had really seen his eyes. They were brown with flecks of green, as if they belonged in a magical forest.

He signaled to his assistant to put on some music. Without saying a word, he put his hand on her back and waltzed her around the circle. Rebecca didn't look down at her feet. She just went where he guided her. She didn't step on his toe once. When it was over, he stopped and bowed to her.

The whole thing had probably lasted no more than seven seconds, but to Rebecca she felt ten feet tall, as if she had grown seven inches for every second.

Finally, Mr. DePalma broke the silence. "What's your name?" he asked, still holding onto her hand.

"Rebecca," she stammered.

"Rebecca," he repeated. The way her name sounded when he said it sent shivers through Rebecca's body. "Rebecca, we exchanged no words, but what did you understand when I stood in front of you?"

Rebecca felt how hot her face had gotten. She could hardly breathe. She wanted to burst out and shout, "*I understood that you love me!*"

"You were asking me to dance," Rebecca mumbled.

"Exactly right—and we did it all without words," said Mr. DePalma. "Dance is *all* body language and it begins from the get-go. Gentlemen, when you ask a lady to dance, you present yourself. You smile. You don't bring her out in a slouch. You are telling her and the world that you've chosen her."

"Ladies, this is no time for dithering or drifting. You do *not* look around the room to see if somebody better is coming to ask you. You've got a split second to say, Yes or Yes. In this class, the answer is always Yes."

Mr. DePalma led Rebecca back to her place in the circle. Shane shuffled away as if she had cooties. "Hey, Mr. DePalma," yelled out Shane. "You must have a death wish. You picked Killer Dancer."

Mr. DePalma still had his hand in Rebecca's. He looked straight at her. "In my world when we call someone a killer dancer—it's a compliment."

5

No Slimy Guts Pasta!

"**I** think I'll have a Halloween party," Samantha announced, the second week of October.

"Oh, goody," said Rebecca. "I'll help decorate the haunted house. And I'll make a bowl of slimy guts pasta. We'll blindfold everybody and get them to put their hands in it." It was well known that Rebecca's favorite holiday in the world was Halloween.

"No slimy guts pasta!" said Samantha, scornfully. "It's not *that* kind of a Halloween party."

"No slimy guts pasta?" repeated Rebecca.

"No bobbing for apples. No sticking your hand in cold pasta. I've got other games in mind," said Samantha with a sly smile.

"No costumes?" asked Rebecca, disappointed. She couldn't imagine Halloween without costumes.

"Well, I assume everybody will wear costumes. But I don't think you should come as a witch. It's time that you break old patterns."

"I not only break patterns, I break toes. But I've always gone as a witch for Halloween. I've got the whole thing—pointy hat, fake nose with warts on it . . ."

"Exactly my point," said Samantha. "You don't want to look like a witch when we play . . . you know."

"You know, what?" asked Rebecca.

"Kissing games," said Samantha. Rebecca unconsciously rubbed her lips with her hand. Samantha laughed. "You know everybody that I invited did that."

"Did what?" asked Rebecca.

"Touched their lips when I said we'd play kissing games."

"Did you actually tell everyone you invited that we were going to play kissing games?" Rebecca asked incredulously.

Samantha giggled. "Yeah," she said. "It was a little embarrassing. I know I blushed when I invited the boys. That's why it's so important we get this first party with kissing games out of the way. We really should have been playing long before this."

The next day at school, Scott came up to Rebecca. "Are you going to Samantha's Halloween party?"

"Of course," said Rebecca.

Scott rubbed his hand over his lips. "Did she tell you she wants to play kissing games?" he asked.

Rebecca nodded. She giggled.

"What's so funny?" Scott asked.

"Samantha said that whenever she mentioned kissing games people touched their lips—and you just did it."

Scott looked appalled, and Rebecca felt bad that she had embarrassed him. "It's okay. I did it, too. Are you going as a vampire?" she asked. Ever since Scott was in third grade he dressed as a vampire for Halloween, just like Rebecca always came as a witch.

"I vill be your vampire and dreenk your blood," Scott said in his fake Transylvanian accent.

"Maybe I'll be a vampire, too," said Rebecca.

"You always come as witch." Scott looked surprised.

"Time to break old patterns," said Rebecca, realizing that she was sounding like Samantha. Still, maybe Samantha had a point. Rebecca thought about the fake nose with the warts on it. "Samantha says I should wear something different. Maybe I'll come as a vampire, too. You always look like you're having fun as a vampire."

"Being a vampire isn't all fun and games," said

Scott, sounding serious. "For example, as a vampire, I have the power of life and death over you. . . ."

"In your dreams, vampire," joked Rebecca.

"Being a vampire is serious business," reprimanded Scott.

"Okay," said Rebecca, trying hard not to giggle.

"As a vampire," continued Scott. He was looking at Rebecca intensely.

"Yes?" said Rebecca.

"I can grant you three wishes that would make your life perfect. What would they be?" Scott asked. Rebecca blushed. He had surprised her. She hadn't imagined that question coming—not in a million years. She couldn't tell exactly if Scott was teasing, or if he expected her to take his question seriously.

"Wouldn't I have to be a vampire in order for you to grant me the wishes?" Rebecca mused, trying to buy time and feeling uncomfortable.

Scott shook his head. "Naw . . . forget it."

"No . . . Scott . . . I . . ." Rebecca felt she had done something to annoy him, but she wasn't exactly sure what. "Let's make *me* the vampire with the power over life and death. What would *you* want?"

"No fair," laughed Scott. "It was my question first."

Rebecca shook her head. "Scott, you're being weird."

"Is weird bad?" asked Scott.

"No," said Rebecca. "I've known you too long to be weirded out—but you're definitely more weird than usual."

"So what would make your life perfect?" Scott asked.

Rebecca thought of the words "Mr. DePalma," but she had a feeling that might hurt Scott's feelings. "You know, I don't know," she said seriously.

Scott shrugged his shoulders. "I don't, either," he admitted. "I'm not even sure I'd like everything perfect."

"Why did you ask, then?"

"I was curious. Lately, I can't figure out what you want," Scott said. Only later did Rebecca realize that it never occurred to her to ask him why it mattered.

Live with It!

After a month of dance classes with Mr. DePalma, everyone in class had learned the basic steps. They had switched partners every few minutes. Now that was all about to change.

"All right, everybody, I want you to line up by height from the smallest to the tallest: girls in one line—boys in another."

Everyone looked at each other in horror. Somehow, this seemed even worse than when he had them stand girl-boy, girl-boy. At least that had been random. Most of the kids in class hadn't been forced to line up by height since second grade, when teachers used it as a means of keeping track of everybody.

At first Mr. DePalma didn't even bother to explain *why* he wanted them lined up that way. There was a lot of jockeying for position, particularly among the boys. They clearly felt it would be an insult to be in any position except tallest.

For the girls, it was just the opposite. Except for a few very short girls, it was better to be small, cute, and compact. Rebecca stood awkwardly toward the back, letting the group in front of her sort itself out. To her surprise, she looked around and noticed that there were quite a few girls who *were* taller than she was. Rebecca found herself in the last third of the line. Adrienne was behind her, just slightly taller than Rebecca.

Mr. DePalma stood at the head of the line. "In dance competitions it looks better if the partners are about the same height. Each pair is going to be a team, and although we will occasionally switch partners in class, the partner you are paired with will be your partner until the final competition."

"You're kidding! What if we don't like the person?" shouted out Shane.

"This isn't about liking or not liking," said Mr. DePalma in his deepest voice. "You are a team. You are not girlfriend and boyfriend. It's like a basketball team or a soccer team. You may not like everyone on your team—but the only way you win is by bringing out the best in each other. In dance, the teams are just two people. And by the way, this is it! Nobody changes partners for any reason. There is no court of appeals. If you think you dance better than your partner, then it is your job to help your partner. Absolutely *no* changing partners. Live with it!"

The thought of being stuck with one partner for every dance class was so horrific that a complete silence fell across the room. Mr. DePalma counted them off, girl-boy, girl-boy. Rebecca eyed the boys' line as it moved forward. The partners who were paired off stood awkwardly with each other. Samantha was partnered with Danny. She made a face, but she didn't say anything.

Rebecca was aware that both Shane and Scott were still in the boys' line, opposite her. Mr. DePalma tapped Rebecca on the shoulder. Then he tapped Scott. Behind them, Adrienne and Shane were paired together.

It was too much for all the kids who knew that Rebecca had once broken Scott's toe. Daniel shouted out, "Mr. DePalma! It's cruel and unusual punishment for Scott to have to dance with Rebecca. She broke his toe dancing with her last year! He's just barely getting over his limp now."

Mr. DePalma looked angry. "I told you. When I give someone a partner it is only because they are about the same height and that looks better to the judges for competition. I don't want to hear one more word about anybody's partner."

Mr. DePalma sounded so angry. Rebecca wondered if he was annoyed because she had caused a disruption in the class. She was so busy worrying about Mr. DePalma that she didn't even notice that Scott himself had not objected to having Rebecca as his partner.

"I'm sorry you got stuck with me," Rebecca whispered to him.

"Forget it," said Scott with a smile. "I'll just wear shoes with steel toes."

Mr. DePalma came over and corrected the way they were standing. He put his hand on Scott's back and pushed him a step closer to Rebecca. "Closer," he said. "I want to see your toes touching at the beginning of the dance. Your arms should be elbow to elbow. Today we'll start with the merengue."

He turned to the class. "Does anybody know where the merengue comes from?"

"Cuba," shouted out Adrienne.

Mr. DePalma shook his head.

"Brazil," offered Adam, a boy in eighth grade.

"Argentina," Samantha called out.

"The island of Merengue," Daniel guffawed.

Mr. DePalma shook his head.

"The Dominican Republic," Scott said softly.

Mr. DePalma nodded. "Very good. The merengue

is one of the easiest dances to learn. It has a simple beat. You just move sideways. The boy lifts his arm, and the girl goes under it. Then the girl lifts her arm, and the boy goes under hers. The movement is all in the hips. But in order to get your hips to move, you have to bend your knees."

He went and put on the music. Scott put his left hand around Rebecca's back. Rebecca took his right hand, and they moved close together so their fore-arms were touching from their elbows to their wrists.

"How did you know it was from the Dominican Republic?" Rebecca asked.

"From my music," Scott answered.

They began to dance. They moved sideways around the floor. Without even realizing it, they swayed their hips with the music. Rebecca's left hip would jut out, just as Scott's right hip did. And then they reversed it. Their upper bodies were relaxed and still. Scott counted the beats out loud. Slowly as they danced they began to drift a little apart, until there was enough light showing through them that another person could have easily slipped in that space.

Mr. DePalma put one hand on Scott's back and one on Rebecca's and pushed them closer together.

"Remember—toes touching, elbows touching, except when you turn."

Rebecca beamed up at Mr. DePalma. "I like your smile, Rebecca," said Mr. DePalma. "It's got a lot of energy in it. Just put that energy into your feet. With a smile like that you'll impress the judges." He patted her on the shoulder as he moved on to another couple.

"He likes my smile," Rebecca gushed to Scott.

Scott was still counting out the beat. "Can you stop talking, please?"

"I think we're supposed to be able to talk and dance at the same time," said Rebecca.

"Not at the beginning," said Scott. "Concentrate."

Rebecca looked down at her feet. "Okay."

"Ladies and gentlemen!" shouted Mr. DePalma. "Move your hips. You are not robots dancing. The judges do not like to watch robots, and neither do I. You are human beings who have hinges. It's a simple rhythm—one, two, one, two."

With the very next one-two, Scott stepped on Rebecca's foot. "Sorry," he apologized.

"It's okay." Rebecca noticed Scott's palm felt sweaty. They kept dancing. Rebecca started moving her hips a little more loosely, trying to imitate the dancers she had seen on TV.

"Stop wiggling around," said Scott.

Mr. DePalma came over to them. "Very good. But Rebecca, put a little less body language into it. Sometimes less is more. The girl's part is deceptive. Hold your arms more firmly, don't just collapse. You've got muscles in those arms. Use them. No one wants to dance with a wet noodle. You have to give Scott something to react to."

Rebecca felt embarrassed that he had criticized her. She stiffened her arms. "Not too stiff," said Mr. DePalma. "It's got to look natural. You'll get it."

Scott was still looking at his feet. "And Scott, lift your head. Your feet will do what they're told. . . ." Mr. DePalma paused. "It's like when you dribble a basketball. You don't look at your feet or the ball, you do it by how it feels."

"Rebecca's the basketball player, not me," mumbled Scott.

"Okay, what's your sport?" asked Mr. DePalma.

"Drums," said Scott. "I don't really have a sport."

"You're a drummer! Great! No wonder your rhythm is so good. Then you know exactly what I'm talking about. When you use the drum pedal, you don't look down at your feet, do you?"

"Unless I've got a broken toe," said Scott.

"You don't have one now, do you?" asked Mr.

DePalma, sounding concerned.

"No," admitted Scott. "It's healed."

"Good," Mr. DePalma paused. "Look you two, I'm not picking on you. The reason I'm correcting you so much is because I can see already that together you two have something special when you dance. It's the kind of chemistry that makes for a winning combination. I just want to bring your talent out in the open so the judges will see it."

Mr. DePalma went on to the others in the class. "I think he means it," said Rebecca excitedly. "He really thinks you and I could win."

"He called you a wet noodle. He could call you noodle pudding, and you'd still gush about him."

"Just dance," said Rebecca, firmly pushing back at Scott with her arms. "I want to win that trophy."

Scott didn't look up. He was still looking at his feet, counting in his head.

The dance class went by more quickly than Rebecca had ever imagined a class could go. "Very good, girls and boys," said Mr. DePalma. "Have a great weekend. It won't hurt if you practice between now and when you see me again."

"When you see me again." To Rebecca they were the five most beautiful words in the English language. Mr. DePalma came over to Rebecca and

Scott. "I particularly hope you two practice together," he said. "You're very talented."

Samantha was waiting for Rebecca and overheard Mr. DePalma. She pulled Rebecca away from Scott. "Are you coming?" she asked, sounding annoyed.

"One minute," said Rebecca. Rebecca glanced over in the corner of the gym, where Scott was still counting in his head and doing the steps that they had learned in a little box step by himself.

Rebecca left Samantha standing where she was and went back to Scott. She got herself back in position and took Scott's right hand. Scott put his left hand on her back. The music had stopped, but Rebecca was still in Scott's arms as he counted out the beat. She felt his hand putting pressure on her back. He raised his arm and Rebecca moved under it, swaying her hips just slightly. Then she raised her arm, and Scott moved under hers, his hips moving much more smoothly than they had at the beginning. Scott lifted his head and grinned. "We got it finally," he said.

"You're good," said Rebecca.

"So are you," Scott replied. "When you aren't a noodle and you concentrate." They broke apart and gave each other a half bow.

Rebecca went back to Samantha, who was still

waiting with her hands on her hips. "Are you finally ready?" she demanded. "We're going to be late for lunch."

"Did you know that Mr. DePalma thinks that Scott and I have chemistry?" Rebecca burbled. "I think we really have a chance to win that contest. I love to dance."

"Well, I think you and Scott looked silly dancing without music," said Samantha. Rebecca stared at Samantha. She could swear that Samantha sounded jealous, but the idea of Samantha being envious of Rebecca seemed ridiculous. Samantha was the girl who everybody else was jealous of. It didn't work the other way. At least it never had yet.

7

Hula's One Thing— Kissing Is Another

Until the last minute, Rebecca couldn't decide what to wear to Samantha's party. She kept putting off dealing with the problem until it was actually the night of the party. She helped her parents set up the candy for trick-or-treaters. "Shouldn't we check your witch costume and make sure it doesn't need any repairs?" asked her mother.

"I don't know if I want to go as a witch tonight," said Rebecca sulkily.

"What do you mean you don't know?" asked her mother. "You always go as a witch for Halloween."

"Samantha doesn't want to have a typical Halloween party. Samantha thinks that witches are for babies," Rebecca explained.

"Well, *excuse* me," said Rebecca's mom, who was dressed as a witch to greet the kids at the door.

Rebecca shrugged. "I didn't mean you," she soothed. "You make a great witch."

"Thank you," her mom said. "Well, if not a witch, what do you want to be?"

"That's the problem. I don't know," Rebecca responded thoughtfully.

"Well." Her mother scrunched her forehead in concentration. "You might have thought of this sooner, but I think we have a tutu. I bought it at a yard sale." Rebecca's mother was forever picking up old costumes at yard sales, just in case. They came in handy. Rebecca's mother got out the box of costumes and found a pink tutu. "You could go as a ballerina. You love your dance lessons at school."

Rebecca shook her head. "Naw, Samantha always comes as a ballerina."

"How about another kind of dancer?" suggested her mother. "Like a hula dancer?"

"Hula dancer?" repeated Rebecca. "Do hula dancers wear Hawaiian shirts?" Rebecca thought of Mr. DePalma in his Hawaiian shirts. Maybe if she went as a hula dancer, she could tell Mr. DePalma about it, and he'd ask to see her costume.

"I don't think traditionally that they do," admitted Rebecca's mother. "But I bet if you wore one with a grass skirt, you'd look adorable."

Rebecca pulled out a faded Ninja Turtle costume. "I can't believe you've saved all these." She put the turtle costume back. "Hula dancers don't wear grass skirts—they wear skirts made out of a special plant called a ti leaf. I read about it in school for a report."

"Well, for this Halloween we may have to improvise." Rebecca's mother went into their bedroom closet and brought out a great-looking green Hawaiian shirt with black-and-white postcards of Hawaii printed on it. "This belongs to your dad, but he won't mind. And we can make a skirt out of cellophane. You can wear a body suit underneath. It'll look great."

Together, Rebecca and her mother stapled strips of different colored cellophane to an elastic band. When it was finished Rebecca tried on the costume. She swayed her hips like a hula dancer.

"I never knew you could move like that," said her mother, sounding both impressed and a little bit alarmed.

"Mr. DePalma says that when you want to move your hips, you have to start with the knees," said Rebecca. "Less is more."

"Well, you definitely got the moves," her mom murmured. "Let's show your costume to your dad."

Her father whistled when he saw Rebecca. "That looks great on you! I guess I lose my shirt again. Hey, do you know what's black and white and green?"

Rebecca's father loved riddles almost as much as Mr. DePalma did. "No, Dad," Rebecca sighed.

"Skunks fighting over a pickle," said her dad.

Rebecca made a face. "That's a terrible joke," her mom lamented. "No girl wants to hear about pickles or skunks on her way to a girl-boy party."

Rebecca glared at her mother. "Why do you have to call it a *girl-boy* party? That sounds so . . . so . . ." Rebecca couldn't think of one word that would fit.

"Well it *is* a girl-boy party, isn't it?" Rebecca's mom asked.

"Yeah, but we don't *call* them girl-boy parties. It sounds so stupid." Rebecca had finally come up with a word, but she wished she hadn't said it. First of all, it wasn't exactly what she meant, and secondly, her mother hated it when she called things or people "stupid."

Her mother made a face. "You know I hate it when you call something 'stupid,' but that reminds me that I've been meaning to talk to you about something."

"Uh-oh," said Rebecca.

"Why uh-oh?"

"Whenever someone says 'I've been meaning to talk to you about something' it's scary."

"This isn't scary," said her mother. "It was just

something you said about Samantha thinking witches were for babies. I know you're not a baby anymore, but I just want to be sure that at this party, or at any party, you don't do anything you're not comfortable with. We've talked about this many times."

Rebecca rolled her eyes. She knew what "this" was. Both her parents wanted her to wait forever for everything—pierced ears, alcohol, romance. The problem was that the kissing games were about to begin, and there was nothing that could stop them.

"Please . . ." begged Rebecca. "Will someone just drive me to Samantha's party!"

8

Spin the Bottle

Samantha came to the door dressed in black tights, a black leotard and a black tutu. "I'm the black swan," she announced proudly. "I told everyone they didn't have to come in costume, but I knew that some would, and Mom said I would make people feel more comfortable if I dressed up."

"I'm a hula dancer," said Rebecca.

"It's cute," said Samantha. Rebecca wasn't sure that cute was a compliment, especially since Samantha looked so slinky.

Adrienne was carrying a purse with a rubber chicken hanging out of it. She waved it in the air. "I'm a comedian," she said.

"Hey, Rebecca, so you really didn't come as a witch," said Scott. He had his vampire teeth in his mouth and a black cape with the red satin lining.

"I told you, Samantha said that this Halloween isn't supposed to be the same-old, same-old.

50

Although, I am glad you still came as a vampire. It wouldn't be Halloween if you weren't a vampire."

"I liked you as a witch." Scott sounded disappointed. "It was tradition. I'm always a vampire. Samantha's always a ballerina. And you're a witch. I miss you being a witch."

Samantha looked hurt. "I'm not just a ballerina. I'm the black swan in *Swan Lake*. I've never worn this outfit before."

"It wasn't an insult, Samantha," said Scott, trying to smooth things over.

"Oh, I know," said Samantha cheerily. She went to greet some other guests.

"Hula dancer, huh?" asked Scott, studying Rebecca's costume. Rebecca swayed her hips.

"Cool shirt," said Scott, looking embarrassed.

"It doesn't remind you of skunks or pickles?" asked Rebecca, fiddling with some loose strands of cellophane.

"No," said Scott. They looked around the room. There were very few decorations.

"It just doesn't feel like Halloween," said Scott.

"Well, maybe we can practice dancing together tonight," Rebecca said.

Scott made a face. "It might be weird, doing that

kind of dancing in front of everybody. You've got to count."

Rebecca felt rejected. "I thought you said we were good together."

"Yeah, in school," said Scott.

Samantha came up to them. "Scott, I think I'd like some punch."

"Okay," said Scott. He made a fist and gave Samantha a playful punch on the arm.

Samantha looked annoyed. "Don't be a baby, Scott," she pouted.

Daniel came over holding an empty Coke bottle. He twirled it in his hand. "Anybody have any idea what to do with this?" he asked with a smirk. He put the bottle down on the floor and spun it.

"Spin the Bottle . . . ?" Shane scoffed. "That's for babies. We should play Seven Minutes in Heaven. Now that's a real kissing game."

"What's 'Seven Minutes in Heaven'?" asked Rebecca.

Everybody started snorting and laughing.

"It's the ultimate kissing game," said Shane.

"I've never heard of it, either," whispered Scott.

"We can warm up with Spin the Bottle," said Samantha. "It's the easiest kissing game. Everyone knows the rules."

"You know what kissing game vampires play, don't you?" asked Scott.

"Love at first bite," guessed Rebecca.

Scott nodded. "You got it!" He pretended to bite Rebecca on the neck. She giggled.

"Rebecca and Scott!" broke in Samantha. "Stop fooling around. Come on. Everybody get in a circle." She handed the bottle to Rebecca. "Rebecca, you can go first."

"Me," squeaked Rebecca. "Why me?"

"Because you're my friend," said Samantha. She squeezed in between Rebecca and Scott. "Besides," Samantha whispered to Rebecca in a voice loud enough for Scott and half the circle to hear. "You need the practice." Rebecca was sure her face was turning every shade of red. She wished that Samantha hadn't found it quite so necessary to remind everybody that she was still in need of remedial kissing lessons.

Rebecca brought her hand up her to her mouth and quickly snatched it away. She didn't want to be seen touching her lips. She put her hand on the bottle's neck. It felt sticky. Then Rebecca realized that it was her own hands that were sweaty.

"Will you spin the bottle!" yelled Daniel. "Or lose your turn."

Rebecca did. But the bottle didn't just spin. It zigged and zagged over the concrete floor, skittering as it spun.

"Wow! You must be desperate to be kissed," said Shane. Rebecca didn't take her eyes off the bottle. Finally it settled into a slower spin. The room grew quiet. It stopped at Daniel. Rebecca looked up at him.

Daniel thumped his chest like Tarzan. "And the winner is . . ." he yelled.

"Yeah," said Shane. "Just be sure she doesn't bust your lip—remember who you've got to kiss."

Rebecca would haven given anything not to have to kiss Daniel. The braces on his teeth looked ominous. As she walked toward him, she tried to think of something funny to say that would let everybody know that kissing Daniel was not a big deal. Nothing came to her. Her mind drew a huge blank when faced with Daniel's braced-up teeth.

Rebecca looked down at Daniel and she started to bend toward him for their kiss. Daniel looked up at her—for a second he looked as scared as she felt. This certainly wasn't the special feeling that her parents had told her was supposed to accompany her first real kiss. Rebecca brought her lips down. Daniel's mouth was open.

His braces caught on the tender part of her upper

lip, where it bowed out. Rebecca tasted a fleck of blood on her tongue.

"Ouch!" she cried out involuntarily.

"That's what porcupines say when they kiss," Scott said. Rebecca moved back into the circle, next to Scott. He made room for her. They were both sitting cross-legged and their knees touched. For a second, Scott put his hand down and it rested on Rebecca's knee. He didn't take his hand away.

It was Shane's turn next. He spun the bottle with a practiced flip of his wrist. As it slowed down, it stopped at Samantha. Rebecca was pretty sure that Shane had cheated and nudged it as it had started to slow down.

"Go, Shane!" shouted Daniel. Shane stood up. He put his hand under his armpit and made the disgusting sound that he was so good at.

"*Quel* romantic," said Samantha sarcastically. Shane started to kiss Samantha, but their foreheads clunked together.

"Ouch!" said Samantha, rubbing her head.

"Score another one for the porcupine ouch kisses," said Scott, taking his hand off Rebecca's knee. "Maybe we should play a different game."

Shane tried to get a real kiss from Samantha, but she hunched her shoulders up and kissed him quickly. She moved back to her place in the circle, once again pushing in between Rebecca and Scott.

"Whose turn is it now?" asked Scott.

"Mine," said Samantha. Samantha spun the bottle with a quick flick of her wrist. It didn't jump. It spun on its center as if it were a perfectly designed top. Rebecca watched it slow down. It stopped at Scott. Rebecca blinked. Had she taken her eyes off of it for a second? It had seemed to be going fast—with enough speed for at least another spin—and then it had suddenly stopped.

There were the usual hoots and hollers, but both Samantha and Scott looked less awkward than the rest of them as they stood in the center of the circle. Samantha was three inches shorter than Scott. The top of her head came to his nose. They had the same size difference as Rebecca and Daniel, but Rebecca thought it was unfair. Just because Scott was a boy and taller, it looked right. Rebecca hated that it looked so right.

"Take out your vampire fangs," Samantha ordered Scott. He took them out and put them in his pocket. Rebecca watched as Samantha raised her arms, put them around Scott's neck, and tilted her head. Scott's head leaned down toward her. Their noses didn't even bump.

The wisecracks stopped. Scott and Samantha kissed. Rebecca stopped breathing. She involuntarily brought her fingers up to her own lips and circled her lips with a feathery touch. Samantha's arms pulled Scott closer to her. Her body seemed to fit perfectly into Scott's. Rebecca's eyes were glued on the couple standing in the center of the circle.

"Hey! Are you two going to come up for air?" asked Shane, obviously annoyed.

Scott and Samantha broke apart. Samantha was blushing. She absentmindedly picked up the bottle as if the game was finished.

"I want another turn," said Shane. He sounded hurt.

Samantha acted like she didn't even hear him. Rebecca couldn't believe that she could ever feel sorry for Shane, but she did.

"Come on, everybody. There are tacos in the kitchen," said Samantha. She grabbed Rebecca's hand. "I've got to go to the bathroom," she said. "Come with me."

"Yeah," said Shane, sounding disgusted. "Girls can never go to the bathroom by themselves."

"Oh, Shane, grow up!" said Samantha.

"What about Seven Minutes in Heaven?" asked Shane.

"Don't you want to eat?" Rebecca asked him. "Samantha said there are tacos in the kitchen." Shane headed for the kitchen.

"Thanks," whispered Samantha to Rebecca. "Boys are always more interested in food than kissing, especially Shane. Let's go."

Rebecca followed Samantha into the bathroom. "Thanks for helping me get away from Shane," said Samantha. "I need to catch my breath. He's such a good kisser."

"Shane?" asked Rebecca hopefully.

"Not Shane, silly! Scott."

"Scott," repeated Rebecca. "I thought Shane was your boyfriend."

"Not necessarily," said Samantha. "Tonight may be the night when all that changes." Samantha had not shown the slightest interest in Scott until Rebecca and he had begun to dance so well together. Dancing with Scott was the one thing that Rebecca could do better than Samantha.

"Shane is still your boyfriend, isn't he?" asked Rebecca, still hoping against hope.

"Have you ever kissed Scott?" Samantha continued, as if she hadn't spoken.

Rebecca flashed back to the long-ago date in third grade. Even in third grade Scott had been a good kisser. "Not in a long while," Rebecca admitted.

Samantha grinned to herself. "I think Scott's going to be my new boyfriend. In fact, I'm pretty sure about it."

Rebecca was aware that ever since Samantha and Scott's kiss, she hadn't been breathing right. "What about Shane?" Rebecca realized she was repeating that ridiculous phrase as if it was somehow going to save her.

"Oh, Shane." Samantha sounded disgusted. "Shane is such a child."

"He's older than Scott," Rebecca protested. "Just two weeks ago you were going on and on about how mature he was."

"It's not chronological age that matters," lectured Samantha. "So what about you and Daniel? Did you like kissing him?"

"No!" blurted out Rebecca. "It was disgusting. His braces hurt, and he's got BO."

"Scott smells good," said Samantha. "I think he uses lavender soap."

Rebecca winced a little. Lavender was her favorite color, but she had to admit that she wasn't sure she would know if somebody was using lavender soap or not.

"I thought you said we should both have a fresh

start this year," argued Rebecca. "You've known Scott almost as long as I have. Scott wouldn't be a fresh start for you."

"Oh yes, he would. Scott and I were never girl-friend and boyfriend. This will be new."

"Did Scott say that he wanted you to be his girl-friend?" Rebecca couldn't let it go. She wondered if it really could work just like that. When the evening had begun the planets had been in the right place. Scott was her dance partner and friend. He had never had a girlfriend except for that brief fifteen minutes with Rebecca. Samantha had a boyfriend named Shane, and that suited Rebecca just fine. Then—one kiss, one *stupid* kissing game—and Scott would belong to Samantha.

Samantha answered Rebecca's question. "He let his lips do the talking." She laughed.

Rebecca started biting her own lip. She didn't realize she was doing it until it began to hurt—at the place where Daniel's braces had cut her. When she and Daniel had kissed they were like two porcupines kissing. When Samantha and Scott had kissed it had apparently been something completely different. Rebecca wished that it had been *her* bottle that had stopped at Scott, and Samantha's had missed Scott entirely.

9

It Don't Mean a Thing— If You Ain't Got That Swing

Samantha told everyone who would listen that Scott was her boyfriend. "That kiss at the party sealed it," said Samantha. "Sealed with a kiss," she giggled. "SWAK!" She wrote the initials Scott + Samantha = SWAK! on the outside of her notebook one hundred times. Each SWAK felt like a whack to Rebecca. Rebecca knew that she didn't have a right to be so out of sorts. It wasn't as if Rebecca had any claim on Scott. Fifteen minutes in third grade, one broken toe, a lifetime friendship, and a dance partnership did not mean that Scott belonged to her. Rebecca wondered if she was a bad person, because she was definitely not happy for Samantha and Scott.

As time went by, the only thing that kept Rebecca from being depressed was the dance classes. In dance class, it didn't seem to matter that Scott and Samantha were supposed to be boyfriend and girlfriend. Scott and Rebecca were in their own world when they danced together. They were best at the Latin dances, in which Rebecca could show off her newfound talent for moving her hips.

After Christmas break, Rebecca couldn't wait for classes to begin again.

"All right, girls and boys," said Mr. DePalma in the first class in January. "Today, I'm going to teach you swing. But that doesn't mean you do your own thing." Mr. DePalma was in a great mood.

He gathered the class in a circle around him. "So far this year, you've learned the merengue, fox-trot, waltz, and rumba. That leaves the tango and swing— two of the hardest dances to learn. I'm going to teach you *my* kind of swing. It's not the high, up on your toes stuff that you sometimes see on TV. You kids are going to learn the authentic swing. It came out of the dance halls of Harlem—and you gotta get down. You gotta lower your seat of gravity and let it rip!"

Mr. DePalma demonstrated the first step. "Okay, take your partners—and gentlemen, I want you to strut in. The judges are looking at you from the moment you take your first step. You lower your butts. You bend your knees. You give your lady your hand. Swing your loose hand, snap your fingers to the beat. Ladies, let the judges and the whole world know you are coming onto the dance floor. You take your free hand and wave it in the air. No Queen of England little flutters here. I want you to announce, 'Watch out world! I'm coming onto the floor.' Okay, let's practice our entrances."

The class started heading into the center of the circle, all bumping hips and waving hands, each one trying to outdo the others. Rebecca waved her hand in the air. She loved the jazzy good-time feel of the music. It seemed to be telling her to let go, have fun, and stop thinking. She felt the fast jumpy beat talking to her. She grinned. She couldn't help herself.

"Stop!" shouted Mr. DePalma. "Girls, most of you are waving your hands as if you're in class hoping to be called on. That's not what I want."

"But I thought you said we were supposed to let the judges and the world know about us," Rebecca said defensively.

"Yes—but you're not shoving yourself in the world's face," said Mr. DePalma.

There were a few snickers. "Or falling flat on her face," cracked Daniel.

"Or breaking toes . . . ." added Shane.

Mr. DePalma frowned. "Actually, Rebecca was one of the few who had the right spirit. When you go out into a dance competition, don't think the judges are stupid. You can't fool them. It's not enough to want the judges or your audience to *think* you are enjoying yourself. You have to actually be enjoying yourself. You don't *look* like you're confident. You *are* confident. I'm seeing a lot of showboating out there. That is not what the judges are looking for and it's not what swing is about. Rebecca and Scott, do your entrance for the group."

Scott and Rebecca looked at each other. They felt shy being singled out, but then Mr. DePalma put on the music again. Scott held out his hand to Rebecca.

They walked into the center of the circle, swiveling their hips. Scott's knees were in a crouch and he was almost slinking. Rebecca's hips swung out with the beat. Her left hand waved in the air, as if it were a butterfly having the time of its life.

The class clapped when they finished. "Very good," said Mr. DePalma. "Now, let's go on. I'll show you what we call the basic step-ball-change footwork."

Scott and Rebecca listened carefully and then tried to copy Mr. DePalma's moves exactly. Scott kept counting out the steps. Rebecca followed him, but every time she swung out away from him, she got her left-right-left footwork mixed up.

Mr. DePalma clapped his hands. "Okay, class. Let's try that combination from the top." Rebecca concentrated, but as she came back in, she was on the wrong foot. When Scott tried to make his next move, he jammed into her—stepping on her toe.

Rebecca rubbed her foot, grimacing in pain. "Is this revenge for my breaking your toe last year?"

"No," said Scott. "Try it again."

Rebecca gamely tried again, but they kept making the same mistake over and over. Scott dropped her hand and scowled at her.

Mr. DePalma came over to them. "What's the matter?"

"Rebecca," said Scott. "She keeps making the same mistake. When she swings back into me she's on her right foot instead of her left foot. So when I step forward I step on her."

Mr. DePalma held out his hand. "Rebecca, try it with me." She smiled up at him happily. It was heaven to dance with Mr. DePalma. Mr. DePalma's hand on her back gave Rebecca instant direction. He swung her out, but when she came back, she realized that she was on the wrong foot again. However, Mr. DePalma did a quick step-ball-change with his own feet and shifted so that with their next move they were in sync again.

He stopped. "Did you both see what I did?"

"Yeah," Scott said. "You did some fancy footwork and you covered for her."

Mr. DePalma shook his head. "No, Scott, you got it wrong, and if you think that way, you'll never get anywhere as a dance team. As partners, if one of you makes a mistake, you don't drop hands and glare at each other. Nobody wins a competition that way. True partners help each other. If one of you makes a mistake, then the other one had better be alert enough to follow that mistake."

"I don't get it," said Scott belligerently. "You *do* mean cover for her—just like I said."

"That's not what Mr. DePalma means," objected Rebecca. "We're a team, it's like covering for someone on the basketball court if they're double-teamed. Or going up for the rebound if one of your teammates shot an air ball."

"Exactly," said Mr. DePalma. "And I need to see more of that teamwork from the two of you. You're very good together. I've got great hopes for the two of you for the citywide contest. Something clicks between you. Rebecca, you give Scott a looseness and lightness that he needs. Scott, you've got the rhythm down pat—but you can be stiff. Loosen up."

Mr. DePalma walked away. Rebecca followed

him with her eyes. "Goo-goo eyes," muttered Scott.

Rebecca glared at him. "I was *not* making goo-goo eyes."

"It was a joke," said Scott.

"Not a nice one," Rebecca snapped. "Maybe you could loosen up more if you were *Samantha's* dance partner." As soon as Rebecca said those words, she wished she could take them back.

"Mr. DePalma said that nobody can change partners," said Scott. Was that a bit of relief she detected?

Of course, Rebecca couldn't leave well enough alone. "Well, we could ask Mr. DePalma if he would make a special exception . . ."

"Will you just shut *up* about it!" insisted Scott.

"Okay," said Rebecca, amazed at just how happy it made her to shut up about it.

Mr. DePalma went to the CD player. "Okay class, you can take a short break for five minutes," he announced. "But I'll keep the music on for any of you who want to keep dancing just for fun."

"Do we have to dance with our official partners?" asked Samantha.

"No," said Mr. DePalma.

Rebecca looked at Scott. Lots of kids were flopping along the sides of the gym, taking breaks. "Do you want to bag it?" she asked him.

"Is that what you want to do?"

"If that's what you want."

"That's a stupid answer."

"Thanks for calling me stupid. I'm not stupid." Rebecca now realized why her mother hated it when she used that word.

"I didn't say you were stupid, but why can't you just say what you want to do? Do you want to keep practicing or not?"

Rebecca paused. It would be so easy to say no and just flop in a corner. Then she would leave the dance floor to Samantha and Scott. But she knew that wasn't what she wanted to do. "Let's try the swing step again," Rebecca held out her hand. Scott took it and started counting out the beat.

"Hey, you two teacher's pets," said Daniel. "Why don't you take a break?"

Scott tripped. Rebecca steadied him with her hand. "Ignore him."

"Right," said Scott. "Let's try that in-out move again."

Scott spun Rebecca out, but he let go of her hand too quickly, and she did an extra turn. But she didn't stop, and when she finished her second turn, Scott was waiting for her. They continued dancing.

Scott was looser now. His limbs moved freely

with the beat instead of the usual stiff way, when he counted it out. When Rebecca made a mistake the next time, he shifted his weight and they were on the right foot again. Scott grinned. It felt good to keep going.

They worked up a sweat, but they no longer had to concentrate quite so hard on every move. They even improvised a little double-step-ball-change that Mr. DePalma hadn't taught them. Through it all, they kept beat.

Rebecca spun out at his signal and waved her free hand in the air. Scott held on to her hand and danced away from her. Because they could trust each other not to let go, they could both lean out. Rebecca could feel the strength in her arm from basketball, and she knew that there was no danger of Scott letting go either.

Scott drew her back in. This time again he was on the wrong foot, but Rebecca quickly shifted and they were right again. "You know, this is fun," beamed Scott. "It really is."

Rebecca couldn't have agreed more.

10

Romeo, Romeo, Wherefore Art Thou?

Rebecca's birthday was on February 15th, right after Valentine's Day. When she had been younger, combining her birthday with a Valentine's party had been kind of fun. There were always chocolate hearts and candies. Naturally, her mother would put up heart decorations everywhere.

This year the last thing Rebecca wanted was a Valentine's party on her birthday. Whenever her mother brought up the subject, Rebecca tried to change it. Finally, she tentatively said, "Maybe we should skip a party this year."

"What! This year you turn thirteen! That's the age that Juliet fell in love with Romeo. Thirteen is a big birthday. We have to celebrate!"

"I don't want that stupid Valentine box you always bring out and the Valentine's cake and all those hearts everywhere. How about pickled, shriveled hearts?"

Rebecca's mother perked up. "That's not a bad idea!"

"Pickled hearts?"

"No, we can have Halloween in February. We'll invite everyone to a monster mash. It'll be kind of an Anti-Valentine's dance. Doesn't that sound like fun?"

Rebecca had to admit it did. "Black hearts," she suggested. "Monster mashed potatoes."

"The reprise of slimy guts pasta!" said her mom. "Let's go to the party store. Maybe they still have a few Halloween decorations. And I bet if they do, they'll be on sale." Rebecca's mother loved nothing as much as a bargain.

"If they have any left," said Rebecca.

"Oh, they will. Let's go." When Rebecca's mother was in a party-giving mode, there was no stopping her. They drove to the mall. "You go into the party store and start looking around," said her mom. "I've got an errand I have to do."

"What's that? I can go with you."

"Not for this one," said her mom.

"Oh, my birthday present." Rebecca smiled.

Her mother raised her eyebrows. "Go on. I'll meet you in about a half hour." Rebecca went into the party store. It was almost sickening how full of romantic Valentine's Day decorations it was.

"You don't have any monster decorations left over from Halloween, do you?" Rebecca hesitantly asked the clerk. He directed her to a bin at the very back of the store. Rebecca was bending over it when she heard a voice that made her jump and spin around. Whenever Rebecca saw a teacher out of context it was always a shock. It never seemed to get easier. A teacher at the movies, a teacher at McDonald's, a teacher with her husband, it always felt weird. But seeing Mr. DePalma was the weirdest of them all.

Even though it was February, he didn't have a jacket on. He was wearing a white T-shirt and jeans. The muscles in his arms showed even more than they did in school with his Hawaiian shirts. He saw Rebecca staring at him and smiled. "Hey, Rebecca," he greeted her.

Rebecca was holding a string of skeletons. "Hi, Mr. DePalma," she said. "What are you doing here?" Rebecca felt like kicking herself. Her voice sounded so phony.

"Just picking up some decorations for my studio. The Dance Center is in this mall," said Mr. DePalma. "By the way, outside of school, I think you can call me Bruce. I'm not *that* much older than you. When I give lessons at the dance center, all my students call me Bruce."

Mr. DePalma looked at the glow-in-the-dark skeletons she was holding. "Isn't it a little late for Halloween?"

"This year I'm kind of having an Anti-Valentine's party. My birthday's near Valentine's Day and ever since I've been a kid, we had the traditional kind of Valentine's birthday party. But this year, I wanted something different." Rebecca was babbling so badly she wanted to stick a sock in her mouth. Besides, she knew adults always laughed in that patronizing way whenever someone her age talked about when they were a kid.

But Mr. DePalma didn't laugh at her. "A monster mash Valentine's Day party," he repeated thoughtfully. "It sounds like fun." He fingered the skeletons dangling from Rebecca's hand. "Will the skeletons be playing the trom*bones*?" Rebecca laughed as if that were the funniest pun she had ever heard.

Just then, a friend of Mr. DePalma's came over carrying a bunch of paper hearts. "Paul, meet Rebecca," said Mr. DePalma. "She's the one I've been telling you about from the William T. Harris Middle School."

Rebecca's mouth dropped open. She couldn't believe the words that she had just heard. Mr. DePalma had been talking about her. What had he been saying?

"Hi, Rebecca," said Paul cheerfully, holding out his hand. Rebecca tried to juggle the skeletons into her left hand so she could shake his hand.

"Rebecca's throwing an Anti-Valentine's Day bash," said Mr. DePalma, as he picked up the skeletons. Paul was almost as good-looking as Mr. DePalma.

"Sounds like fun," said Paul, as he leaned over and shook Rebecca's hand. They were both treating her as if she were so grown-up. Then he said the words that exploded in Rebecca's heart. "You're every bit as pretty as Bruce said you were."

"And wait till you see her dance," said Mr. DePalma, oblivious to the potential heart attack he was causing. "Well, we'd better get going. Rebecca, I'll see you at school."

"Good-bye, Mr. DePalma . . . uh . . . uh . . . Bruce!" stammered Rebecca. Mr. DePalma gave her one of his gorgeous smiles.

Rebecca stayed rooted to the spot. Her mom came into the store. "Hi, honey. Who were those great-looking men I saw you talking to?" she asked, as she looked over Rebecca's choices.

"That was Mr. DePalma my dance teacher, and his friend," said Rebecca.

Rebecca's mom grinned. "Well, no wonder . . ."

"No wonder *what?*" asked Rebecca.

"No wonder, he's all I hear about. He's gorgeous."

"Mom!" said Rebecca. She didn't like hearing her mom talk about Mr. DePalma being gorgeous.

"What?"

"You shouldn't talk about my teachers like that . . . and besides Dad wouldn't like it."

Rebecca's mom laughed. "I don't think your dad would mind. Just because I'm married doesn't mean that I can't appreciate a good-looking man. You'll find out when you're older."

"Mom!"

"You're right. I'm sorry. I used to hate it when adults told me that I'd find out when I'm older. Forgive me?"

Rebecca shrugged. "Sure." She just wanted her mom to shut up. She wanted to be alone with her thoughts. What was it that Mr. DePalma had said? *She's the one I've been telling you about.*

What could that mean? Teachers weren't allowed to be in love with their students. Mr. DePalma might have talked to his friend about the fact that he was willing to wait until Rebecca was old enough to be a true partner.

Mr. DePalma's friend had said, *You're every bit as pretty as Bruce said you were.*

It isn't a fantasy, thought Rebecca breathlessly. Mr. DePalma really is in love with me! Stranger things had happened. Shakespeare had written about it. Songs had been sung about it. In just a few weeks Rebecca would be exactly the same age as Juliet. If she wasn't too young for Shakespeare, she wasn't too young for Mr. DePalma.

That's Girl Power

**WHAT DID THE MONSTER TAKE
TO THE VALENTINE DANCE?**

His Ghoul Friend.

Celebrate Rebecca's birthday at a
MONSTER MASH.

February 14, 7 PM

Slimy Guts Pasta and
Monster Mashed Potatoes
will be served.
Come as your favorite monster.
42 Liberty Street
RSVP

"Cool invitation," Scott complimented her at school.

"Yeah," said Rebecca. "You get a chance to wear

your vampire costume twice in one year."

"Maybe I won't come as a vampire," mused Scott. "I might make a good-looking ghost."

"That's pretty conceited of you," laughed Rebecca. "What makes you think you're going to come back any more handsome as a ghost?"

"Because I'd be very *haunt*some," said Scott. He pointed his finger at her. "Gotcha!"

"Very funny." Rebecca took his finger and pointed it back at Scott. "You're getting so conceited, your idea of a real treat is to stand in front of the mirror and look at yourself!"

"Hey, I'm not really that conceited, am I?" asked Scott, sounding worried.

"Well, no," Rebecca admitted. Scott was good-looking, but he wasn't really conceited.

"Thanks," said Scott. "Hey, do you want to practice dance together this weekend? Maybe Sunday."

"Sure," said Rebecca, pleased that Scott had asked. "We can do it at my house."

"Great." Scott left to go down the hall. Rebecca couldn't help smiling to herself. Samantha came up to her.

"I got your invitation," said Samantha. "But I don't get it. Why are you having a costume party around Valentine's Day?"

Rebecca hesitated. She didn't want to say, "Because I thought your Halloween party was so lame." Instead, Rebecca just shrugged. "You know my mom. Any excuse to decorate."

"Well, I don't know what to go as," said Samantha.

"How about the Bride of Frankenstein," suggested Rebecca. "*Roses are red, Four-leaf clovers are green. When I see your face, I want to scream.*"

"That's not a bad idea," said Samantha. "Not the poem. The idea of being the Bride of Frankenstein. I could put white stuff on my hair and wear it really wild—but kind of pretty. Who are you going to be?"

"I guess I'll wear my witch's costume," said Rebecca. She remembered Scott telling her that he had missed her as a witch.

"I know the perfect game that we absolutely *have* to play at your party."

"Pin the tail on the monster?" asked Rebecca.

Samantha made a face. "No . . . it's called Seven Minutes in Heaven."

"Oh, yeah," said Rebecca. "I remember Shane talking about it, but I don't know how to play."

"I've been doing research," said Samantha, leaning in conspiratorially. "It's a truth-or-dare game. You ask a boy a question, and he can either answer it with the whole truth or you go alone into the closet with him and lock lips for seven minutes. That's a *real* kissing game."

"Seven minutes is a long time," said Rebecca, beginning to panic. She involuntarily looked down at her watch. "How can you breathe?"

"You practice," said Samantha, as if it were a skill that could be easily learned, like swimming underwater.

"What happens if you have to kiss somebody you don't want to?"

Samantha giggled. "Well, it's your job to make sure that doesn't happen. That's girl power." Samantha put her arm around Rebecca comfortingly. "Don't worry about it."

Rebecca tried not to worry. She figured the best way not to worry would be not to think about it at all.

12

It Doesn't Add Up

On Sunday afternoon Rebecca waited at home for Scott. She put on the practice tape that they had gotten from Mr. DePalma and worked on the steps alone, dancing around the living room. She held her left arm up at shoulder level as if it were resting on Scott's shoulder; her right arm was up at a right angle. She moved around the living room, carefully avoiding the coffee table, counting out the steps for the fox-trot. Quick, quick—slow. Quick-quick—slow.

She didn't even realize that her father had come into the room and had been watching her from the corner. "Do you need a stand-in partner?" he asked. Her father held his arms open for her. "Come on, give your old man a try." Rebecca put her hand on his shoulder. They did the fox-trot, and she was able to follow every move that her father made. Every change of direction that he was going to make, she felt from his hand on her back. She had never realized before that her father was a good dancer.

"When you were little, you used to look at your feet whenever we danced," said her father. "I could never get you to raise your head."

"That's because I was dancing on your feet. Didn't it hurt?"

"No," said her father. "Well, maybe when you were about ten at your cousin Dana and Pat's wedding. That was the first time you insisted on wearing shoes with little heels. Still, I always loved dancing with you on top of my shoes."

"Mr. DePalma says that dancing should be four feet pretending to be two, the way it was when I was on top of your shoes."

"Not just *pretending* to be two. When dancing works, four feet *are* two. You listen to your partner. You listen to the music. You're not listening with your ears, but with your body. Dancing is as much about listening and being still as it is about moving."

"Dad!" exclaimed Rebecca. "You sound just like Mr. DePalma."

"Well, I took dance lessons myself, you know. Your great-grandmother made me. She paid for lessons because she wanted me to be able to dance with my sister."

"Was that my great-grandma Becky? The same one who didn't like to go backward?" asked Rebecca. "The one I'm named after?"

"Exactly. She was a great dancer herself. Dancing was the only time that you could get that dame to go backward, and even then she didn't like it. My grandfather used to complain that she was always trying to take the lead."

Rebecca made a little face. "Sometimes, Scott and I get tangled up because I take the lead."

"Well, it's hard to learn to take signals, but you're doing just fine now." He twirled her around the floor. "You know what I love about dancing? It's that you can never tell by just looking at people who's going to be the good dancer. It isn't always the best-looking ones or the ones with the best bodies."

"I think I surprised a lot of people," said Rebecca. "You wouldn't know from looking at me that I'm a good dancer."

Her dad chuckled. "Maybe you'll be the dance champion in the family."

"I thought you wanted me to be a basketball star."

"I want you to follow your talents wherever they take you. By the way, put strength back in your arms. You've got to hold your own when you dance."

"That's what Mr. DePalma says."

"Well, then it must be right," teased her father. "If I had a dollar for every time you said, 'The gorgeous Mr. DePalma says . . .'"

"I don't call him 'the gorgeous Mr. DePalma!'" protested Rebecca. "How do you know he's gorgeous?"

"Your mom told me." Just then the doorbell rang. Rebecca's dad bowed to her. "Thank you for that charming dance, Miss Rebecca." She curtsied to him.

Rebecca went to the door and let Scott in. He looked like he was in a bad mood. Scott's cellular phone rang. He ignored it. "Don't you want to answer it?" Rebecca asked.

Scott shook his head.

"What if it's your parents?" Rebecca asked. Rebecca knew that Scott's parents had gotten him the phone with the rule that he wasn't allowed to give the number out to his friends.

"Let's practice," said Scott. "And not talk."

"Okay." Rebecca was in a good mood. She put the tape back on, then walked over to Scott and put her hand on his shoulder. They started to do the box step, alternating it with a promenade where they moved sideways across the room.

"I was practicing with my dad," said Rebecca.

"He's good. The great-grandmother that I'm named after paid for him to take lessons. Isn't that neat? I bet Mr. DePalma will be interested. Maybe I'll bring him the picture of my great-grandmother in her Model T Ford. Did I tell you that I ran into Mr. DePalma? It was so cool. Mom and I were shopping for decorations for my birthday party. He was so nice. He wanted me to call him Bruce after school . . ."

Scott stopped dancing. "Can't you ever be quiet?" he demanded. "What is it with you girls? Your mouths just keep going!"

Rebecca blinked. She was hurt. "What did I do?" Scott's cellular phone rang again. He picked it up and turned it off so it wouldn't ring. A few seconds later, Rebecca's home phone rang.

"Rebecca!" shouted her father. "It's Samantha. Do you want me to tell her you'll call her back?"

"Let's keep practicing," said Scott.

"Tell her I'll phone her later," Rebecca called out.

Her father came back into the living room carrying the phone. "She says it's important."

Rebecca went to pick up the receiver. Scott grimaced. "Hi," whispered Rebecca into the phone. "I can't talk too long."

"Is Scott there?" asked Samantha. She sounded

close to tears. Scott was shaking his head and waving his hands in front of him.

"Uh . . ." said Rebecca. "We're practicing."

Scott gave Rebecca a rather disgusted look.

"Can I talk to him?" Samantha pleaded. "I know he's there."

Rebecca handed the phone to Scott. She shrugged. "She knows you're here," she whispered to Scott.

Scott scowled as he turned and took the phone. "Look, I can't talk. I told you. Good-bye." He hung up and gave the portable phone to Rebecca. She put it down on the couch and stared at it.

"Samantha sounded upset," said Rebecca. "Did you two have a fight?"

"Do you want to practice or not?"

"But you practically hung up on Samantha. I think you should call her back."

"No," said Scott.

"But I thought you and she were boyfriend and girlfriend—although you never seem to do things together. I don't get it."

"I'm out of here," said Scott abruptly. "I'm going to go practice my drums. At least that's something that I can do by myself." He picked up his backpack and walked out. Rebecca stood frozen. She couldn't believe that he had run out on her. Maybe he had broken up with Samantha. Rebecca hurried to the phone and called her back.

"What's going on?" she asked. "What happened between you and Scott?"

"Is he still there?" sniffed Samantha.

"No," said Rebecca. "He walked out on me."

"He can be such a jerk," said Samantha. "I called him on his cell phone a half hour ago and he said he couldn't talk."

"What was so important?"

"I'm taking a Valentine's quiz in a magazine. 'How to find out if you're really compatible.' I need to know his favorite animal."

"A worm," said Rebecca.

"A worm?" repeated Samantha. "I don't even think that's on the list of possibilities."

"Well, it's Scott's favorite animal. He likes that they can grow back if you cut them in half. Worms help lawns by making holes. Scott thinks worms get a bad rap. He hates it that calling someone a worm is an insult. He used to collect them."

"Worms?" echoed Samantha incredulously. "So what's his favorite color?"

"That's easy," said Rebecca. "Black. Have you ever seen him in anything other than black jeans?"

"Does he like spicy or bland food?"

"Bland," said Rebecca. "He doesn't even like macaroni and cheese. He's into macaroni and butter."

"Thanks," said Samantha. Samantha hung up. Rebecca looked around the empty room. She realized quite a few things:

1. Scott had given Samantha his cell-phone number.
2. Scott might have hung up on Samantha, but he had walked out on Rebecca.
3. Rebecca knew more about Scott's likes and dislikes than Samantha did.
4. Rebecca hadn't even told Samantha about meeting Mr. DePalma in the mall.
5. Rebecca didn't have the foggiest idea what they all added up to.

T-A-N-G-O

Samantha told everybody that she and Scott had a silly fight, but they were over it. "He said he was sorry—that he just gets into these moods," said Samantha, sighing. "It was kind of cute."

"That's so romantic," said Adrienne. "Having a fight. Making up. I wish I had a real boyfriend like Scott."

"I don't get it," said Rebecca. "You two never see each other outside of school. At least not that I know of. What exactly makes you boyfriend and girl-friend?"

"Well, it's something special," said Samantha. "You know, it's not always easy. I found out when I took that Valentine's quiz that Scott and I have a 'combustible relationship.'"

"What does that mean?" asked Rebecca.

"It means that it can burst into flames at any moment," said Samantha dramatically.

"I know what the *word* means," said Rebecca, getting more annoyed by the second. "It's just that Scott is the least combustible person I know. In fact, the fire department voted him the kid least likely to spontaneously burn."

"When did they hold that contest?" asked Samantha.

"It's a joke," explained Rebecca tiredly.

"What made you so grumpy today?" asked Samantha. "You should be in a good mood. Everybody is talking about you."

"About me? Why?" asked Rebecca.

"Your party, silly," said Samantha. "I told everybody that we are definitely playing Seven Minutes in Heaven at your party. You're so lucky that your birthday is around Valentine's Day."

Rebecca grimaced. She didn't feel lucky. She couldn't believe that Scott had apologized to Samantha for not answering her stupid questions, but he hadn't bothered to ask Rebecca to forgive him for walking out on her. The more Rebecca thought about it, the angrier she became.

Just outside of the gym before dance class, Scott finally came up to her. He could instantly tell she was upset. "I'm sorry I bailed on you," he said quickly.

"You were a worm," whispered Rebecca fiercely.

Scott looked shocked. He wasn't used to seeing Rebecca so mad.

"I said I was sorry."

"Well, sorry doesn't do me much good. You know dancing is important to me. It's my *life*."

"Your life!" said Scott in a mocking voice.

Rebecca was in no mood to be teased. "It stunk the way you just walked out. We have a chance to win that tournament."

"I was just sick of girls," Scott defended himself.

"Thank you very much," said Rebecca. "In case, you forgot, *I* am a girl. And I got stuck having to tell Samantha every stupid thing about you. She's your girlfriend and she didn't even know that your favorite animal is a worm and that you only like spaghetti with butter and no tomato sauce. Yet you had time to tell Samantha you were sorry, and not me."

"She called me at home! She calls me a lot. What was I going to do?"

"I don't know. And I don't care! It's not my problem," said Rebecca. She stomped on to the gym. Mr. DePalma was waiting for them in the gym class. This time he was wearing a deep blue shirt and a dark tie. He had on pressed black pants and black dance shoes. Rebecca looked for a sign that he couldn't take his eyes off her, but he barely glanced at her. This was definitely not a good day.

"All right, everybody. Today, we learn your last dance of the year, the Argentine tango. T-A-N-G-O. The letters give you the beat. Five letters for one of the most beautiful dances in the world. It uses some of the same slow-slow, quick-quick patterns that we've learned before, but the tango is different because of the way you move and the way you relate to each other. In no other dance does the couple have to move so closely together. It comes from a Latin word *tangere*, which means to touch. The tango is a mix of an African slave dance and the Spanish flamenco. It has to have a mix of passion and sorrow. It's a dance full of surprises."

Rebecca hung on every word. Just listening to Mr. DePalma talk about dance lifted her bad mood. The way he spoke about the tango made her want to try it.

"We begin with *El Paseo*, the stroll," said Mr. DePalma. "You are going to be walking counter-clockwise around the edge of the floor. You must follow the line of dance. When you move toward the center, you will be doing what I call 'the scorpion.' You shift directions with your feet, and purposefully walk toward the center. Your hands are above your heads, still clasped together. The girl's arm and the boy's arm form the shape of a scorpion's tail."

"Tigers—scorpions," Shane said loudly. "It sounds like Rebecca's monster mash."

"Well, monsters do dance around Valentine's Day," said Mr. DePalma, giving Rebecca a wink. "Let's begin. Take your partners."

Scott held his hand out to Rebecca. They got into position, but Rebecca was still angry at him. She turned her cheek so that she wasn't looking at Scott. Scott put his hand on her back.

"Ladies and gentleman, begin the Paseo." Mr. DePalma clapped out the beat. Rebecca held her body stiffly. Mr. DePalma came up to them.

"Excellent, excellent," he said. "Rebecca, you're showing the exact kind of controlled passion that the dance requires. And the position of your head is perfect. By looking away from your partner, you give him a clear view of the dance floor, so he can anticipate danger and trouble spots. Then I'll choreograph some head whips just for you. It's part of the drama of the tango."

Mr. DePalma moved on to the next couple. "Oh, no," whispered Scott. "Mr. DePalma used the words 'excellent,' 'passion,' 'perfect,' and 'you' together. Not to mention head whips, whatever they are. You're going to be impossible."

Rebecca refused to answer him. They danced, rocking back and forth to the music, changing directions quickly. Because she wasn't looking at Scott, Rebecca had to pick up clues by feeling Scott's body movements. They seemed to know without speaking what the other was going to do. For several minutes they danced without exchanging a word.

"You know what," said Scott. "You're a lot easier to lead when you're mad at me. You're not a piece of limp spaghetti."

"I have never been limp spaghetti," said Rebecca.

"Yeah, you have been. Not all the time, only sometimes," Scott pointed out, trying to be fair.

His fairness was lost on Rebecca. He was making her so mad that her fingers were like a vise on his shoulders. She shifted toward the center of the circle, ready to do the scorpion, the move where they held their arms over their heads to look like a scorpion's tail.

Scott wasn't expecting her to lead. He tripped on his feet and fell on his butt on the floor. Mr. DePalma came over and helped him up. "What's the problem? You both were looking so good."

"She changed directions on me," scowled Scott. "She doesn't let me lead."

"Scott just keeps doing all the boring steps and

never changes," argued Rebecca.

"Rebecca," said Mr. DePalma, "it's really important that you *not* anticipate what Scott is going to do. Even though it's killing you, you have to let him lead. Stay attuned to what he's doing. In the tango, you resist—just a little—being moved. That makes it more interesting for your partner."

"My partner doesn't like it interesting. He likes his spaghetti bland," Rebecca spat out the words.

Mr. DePalma turned a puzzled look at Scott. "What does this have to do with spaghetti?"

"Nothing," said Scott. "Come on, Rebecca. We'll try it again." He offered Rebecca his hand. "T-A-N-G-O." Scott spelled out the beat the way Mr. DePalma had taught them.

"I didn't appreciate you telling Mr. DePalma that I like bland spaghetti," muttered Scott.

"Well, I didn't appreciate you telling him that I try to lead," mimicked Rebecca.

"Well, you do," said Scott.

"And you like bland spaghetti."

Just then Adrienne and Shane bumped into them. "Whoops," said Adrienne breezily. "Our scorpion got out of hand."

"Maybe I'll come as a scorpion to your Monster Mash," said Shane. "Scorpions like dark places like a closet. Seven Minutes in Heaven, here I come!"

A few seconds later Samantha and Daniel danced by. "I told you everybody's excited about your party, and Seven Minutes in Heaven," whispered Samantha.

"Yeah, can't wait," said Daniel, making disgusting smacking sounds, as he bent Samantha over in a dip.

"What's this Seven Minutes in Heaven again?" whispered Scott.

"It's a game so confusing that it makes chess look simple," said Rebecca in exasperation as they danced. "I think it's a combination of truth or dare and kissing in the closet."

"Have you ever played it?" Scott asked.

Rebecca and Scott were dancing so close that Rebecca's mouth was practically in Scott's ear.

"No," Rebecca admitted.

"T-A-N-G-O," said Scott as he changed direction and they went into the scorpion. "You know," he added, "we're actually getting this dance."

They kept dancing.

"I like spicy food every once in a while," Scott whispered into her ear.

14

Too Many Brides of Frankenstein

On the day of Rebecca's birthday party, Rebecca helped her parents with the spaghetti sauce. "Not too much garlic," Rebecca warned her mother.

"Without garlic, you'll be bitten by a vampire," warned Rebecca's father.

"Dad, please, just don't put too much garlic in the sauce," implored Rebecca.

"I don't get it," said her father. "We always put garlic in our spaghetti sauce, and you never complained before."

"Rebecca will be officially a teenager tomorrow," said her mother. "I think she's entitled to a party without garlic. We'll go easy on it."

They finished the sauce. Rebecca started to clean up. She stood over the sink, letting the water run through her hands. Her mother came and started to dry the big pots. "Rebecca, we want you to have fun tonight. However, I want all your friends to know that your parents are in the house, and we'll come down to see how things are going every now and then."

"Yes, Mom," said Rebecca, secretly a little relieved. She wiped her hands on a dish towel. Seven minutes in a closet seemed like an awfully long time.

"Honey," said her mom, when they finished the dishes. "Maybe this is the time to give you your birthday present."

"Aren't you going to save it for tomorrow on my real birthday?" Rebecca asked.

"We thought you might want to wear it tonight," said her mother.

Rebecca looked puzzled. Her mother knew she was planning on wearing her witch's outfit, which had sat in mothballs during Samantha's party.

Rebecca's mother went into the closet and brought out a long, rectangular box, wrapped in golden paper. It looked expensive.

"What is it?" Rebecca asked.

"Open it," said her mom.

Rebecca tried to take the paper off carefully, but she lost patience and ripped it off. She pushed aside the tissue paper. Inside was the most beautiful dress Rebecca had ever seen. It was white with lavender ribbons daintily circling an empire waist. The scoop neck was lined with eyelet lace.

Rebecca pulled it out reverently.

"Do you like it?" Rebecca's mom asked. "We thought you could wear it tonight, and then wear it to the ballroom dancing contest."

Rebecca nodded, barely able to speak. "It's beautiful," she said. "But I don't see how I can wear it tonight. We told everybody it was a monster mash. Shouldn't I wear my witch's outfit?"

"Well, a witch isn't really a monster," said Rebecca's dad. "And we thought of that. There's a second half to your present." He brought out what looked to be a hatbox.

"A matching hat?" guessed Rebecca.

Rebecca opened the box and gave a little yelp. It looked as if some furry dead gray animal was lying in the box. Her father laughed. He pulled out a gray wig with long, flowing ringlets. Rebecca tried it on.

"With a little white makeup and that wig you'll be the perfect Bride of Frankenstein," said Rebecca's mom. "That way, you can be a monster and still be pretty."

Rebecca tried on the wig. She held the dress up to her body and went to the mirror. The wig didn't make her look spooky. She looked almost glamorous.

"I don't know," she said worriedly. "I think Samantha's coming as the Bride of Frankenstein, too."

"So what? Who said you can't have more than one

Bride of Frankenstein?" asked her father.

"I'm sure there will be more than one Frankenstein and lots of werewolves," said Rebecca's mom. "Let me put your makeup on."

Her mother put pale powder on Rebecca's face and used black eyeliner on her eyes. She took a lip-brush and painted Rebecca's lips with a pale white lipstick. Rebecca looked ghostly, but romantic. The wig gave her a wild look. She slipped on the dress. No Bride of Frankenstein had ever felt as pretty.

The doorbell rang. It was time for the party.

"Wow!" exclaimed Scott when he saw her.

"Double wow!" said Rebecca as she stared at him. "You're not a vampire." Scott had black fake scars running down his face. He was wearing football pads under a jacket that made his shoulders look huge.

"Frankenstein, I presume," said Rebecca.

"The Bride of Frankenstein?" Scott asked.

Rebecca gave him a mock curtsy. "Nobody's going to believe that we didn't plan this."

"I was tired of being a vampire. I thought I'd try another monster. So I came as Frankenstein. It's so funny that you came as the bride."

"Well, you know what the real Frankenstein said when he saw his bride?" asked Rebecca.

"No," said Scott.

"It's love at first fright," said Rebecca. He groaned. Rebecca thought maybe she shouldn't have made that joke. She played nervously with the eyelet lace on the fringe of her neck.

"Seriously, you look terrific," said Scott. He handed her a present. It was clearly a CD.

Rebecca smiled at him. "I'll open it later."

Samantha and Adrienne arrived together. Adrienne took one look at Rebecca and burst out laughing. Adrienne was dressed as a witch, but Samantha was dressed as the Bride of Frankenstein.

"You should have told me that you were coming as the Bride of Frankenstein," Samantha said through clenched teeth. She was wearing a pink nightgown and she had put so much hair spray on her hair that it stuck straight out.

"I didn't know until tonight," said Rebecca. "The dress and the wig were birthday presents from my folks."

"Happy birthday, by the way," said Adrienne. Samantha shoved her present into Rebecca's hands, too. Rebecca thanked them both, but her eyes were on Samantha. Rebecca had a feeling that her father was wrong. There was definitely such a thing as too many Brides of Frankenstein.

15

Seven Minutes in Heaven

Samantha crossed the room to where Scott was looking over the CDs and putting one on. "Hi Scott," she gushed.

"Uh, hi, Samantha," mumbled Scott.

"I think it's so cute you came as Frankenstein!"

"Thanks," said Scott. "What's your costume? Are you supposed to be one of the characters who gets killed in *I Know What You Did Last Summer*?"

"No," snapped Samantha. "I'm the Bride of Frankenstein."

"Oh," said Scott. "You look a little modern."

"Stop being so *literal*, Scott," said Samantha. "Come on, let's dance together. This isn't class. We can dance with whoever we want."

Rebecca watched Samantha and Scott dance together. The CD that Scott had put on was one of the swing songs that Rebecca and Scott had practiced to.

Just then Daniel and Shane came in together. Daniel was dressed as a vampire and Shane as a werewolf.

"Hey, Rebecca," said Daniel. "Knock, knock."

"Who's there?" asked Rebecca suspiciously.

"Lena," said Daniel.

"Lena who?"

"Lena over this way, I want to give you a little kiss."

Rebecca shoved a bowl full of cold spaghetti at him. "Here, cool down, stick your hand in, and feel the guts of a hundred skeletons."

"Skeletons don't have guts. That's why they're afraid to cross the road," said Daniel.

"Hey, I thought we were going to play some real games at this Monster Mash," said Shane. "Not tell stupid jokes."

Rebecca's eyes kept going back to watch Samantha and Scott dancing. They didn't dance particularly close. Scott was doing the box step, but Samantha started off on the wrong foot, and bumped into him. They broke apart.

"Let's not do that silly school stuff," said Samantha. Scott dropped his arms. Samantha started to shimmy and jump up and down even though it wasn't really a rock song.

Rebecca was about to join them, figuring that since they weren't touching, anyone could join in, but Daniel came over to her and put his fake teeth on her neck.

"Daniel!" protested Rebecca, shoving him away.

"Did you hear about the boy vampire and girl vampire who couldn't get married?" asked Daniel.

"No," said Rebecca.

"They loved in vein."

"How about the vampire who went to sea," said Daniel. "He went in a blood vessel."

Rebecca groaned. "Cut it out!" she said.

"Okay," said Daniel. "But remember, you asked me. Now I will have to cut out your heart and eat it." He wiggled his hands at Rebecca's throat.

"When do we start Seven Minutes in Heaven?" demanded Shane.

"Patience, jackass, patience," said Rebecca.

"Who are you calling jackass?" demanded Daniel.

"It's the punch line of a long joke my father tells," said Rebecca.

"I love that joke," said Scott, who stopped dancing with Samantha and came over to them. "A guy and his donkey are crossing the desert. The donkey keeps asking, 'When are we going to get there?'"

"Patience, jackass, patience," giggled Rebecca.

She and Scott had told the joke so often that they knew it by heart.

"They kept crossing the desert," continued Scott. "And the donkey kept asking, 'When are we going to get there?'"

"Patience, jackass, patience," repeated Rebecca.

"But the day got longer and the sun hotter," said Scott dramatically. "And again the donkey brayed, 'When are we going to get there?'"

"Patience, jackass, patience," drawled Rebecca.

Samantha was getting very impatient. "When is this joke going to be over?"

Rebecca and Scott looked at each other and burst out laughing. "Patience, jackass, patience!" they shouted in unison.

Samantha glared at them. "I don't think that's funny."

"That's the point of the joke," explained Scott. "To get somebody to say what you said."

"Oh," said Samantha. "That's so juvenile. I think it's time to play Seven Minutes in Heaven."

16

Apparently Heaven's a Very Funny Place

Samantha's announcement was met with stunned silence. Everybody stared at her.

"What's Seven Minutes in Heaven again?" asked Adrienne.

"Seven Minutes in Heaven just happens to be the hottest game there is," bragged Shane. He waved his hand in the air as if the heat was too much for him. Then he put his hand on his armpit and let loose one of his patented disgusting sounds.

"That's very attractive," said Samantha.

Scott made a face. "Will somebody explain the rules to me?"

"The simplest way is just to play and then you'll get it," said Samantha.

"Okay, so, Samantha, why don't you start?" said Shane in a taunting voice. Rebecca breathed a sign of relief. She wasn't sure that she really understood how the game worked, and she knew that she didn't want to go first.

"Uh, just one thing," said Rebecca. "My folks are upstairs. They might come down anytime, so we probably can't play unless the closet door stays open a crack."

"Okay," said Samantha, taking center stage. "I get to ask anybody a question. It can be about anything. Actually, in this game the question isn't really that important. The person answering has two choices. They can answer the question. Or, if they want, they can go in the closet with the person who asked them for seven minutes."

"What do you do in the closet for seven minutes?" asked Scott.

The whole party broke up laughing hilariously, as if he had just said the funniest thing in the world.

"That's why they call it *heaven*," shouted out Shane.

"Okay, I'll start it off," said Samantha. "Now, remember, the person I pick doesn't have to answer the question. They might prefer the . . ."

"*We get it*, Samantha," said Daniel impatiently. "They might prefer to go into the closet with you. Just ask your question."

"Okay . . ." said Samantha, looking a little

uncomfortable. "This question is for Scott." She smiled at him. "What is your favorite animal?"

"A worm," Scott said quickly.

The group burst out laughing. Daniel made clucking sounds. "I think his favorite animal is a chicken!"

Samantha turned several shades of red. "Maybe Scott didn't understand."

"He understood," said Shane. "My turn. Okay, Rebecca? It's your party." Rebecca nodded, trying not to show how relieved she was that Scott had chosen to answer the question instead of being locked in a closet with Samantha for seven minutes.

Shane stood in front of Samantha. "My question is for Samantha. How come you dropped me for Scott?"

The room grew quiet. Samantha blinked.

"She doesn't have to answer that," said Rebecca quickly. It seemed like an unfair question to ask Samantha in front of everybody. If Shane had really wanted to know, he should have asked Samantha a long time ago.

"Right," said Shane. "She doesn't have to answer. That's the point of the game. She can tell the truth or take the consequences. She can go in the closet with me."

Samantha bit her lip. She looked across the circle at Scott. She started to get up and walk into the closet. Shane clapped his hands over his head as if he was the champion.

Then Samantha stopped. "Because Scott is a better dancer," she answered. "And a great kisser." Samantha walked away from the closet. There were a lot of nervous laughs. Shane tried to look as if it didn't matter, but you could tell he was crushed.

"Hey, Rebecca!" Adrienne shouted. "It's your party. How come you haven't taken a turn? You should play on your birthday!"

"Yeah, Rebecca. Who do you want to go in the closet with?" asked Daniel. He made chopping noises with his teeth.

Rebecca looked around the circle. Her eyes fell on Scott. She really wanted to kiss him. Even before Samantha had kissed him playing Spin the Bottle, she had wanted to be able to kiss Scott—and not like a third-grade kiss.

"Okay," said Rebecca. She looked around the room. "This is for Scott. I can grant you three wishes to make your life perfect. What would they be?"

"Go on, Scott," shouted Daniel. "Tell her the truth. You're life would be perfect if you could get out of dancing with Killer Dancer."

Scott made a face. "That's not it," he said.

"Well, answer her," said Samantha.

"Yeah, Scott. Better answer her," said Shane. "Otherwise you have to go into the closet with Rebecca. Who knows what limb she might break in the dark?"

Still Scott didn't answer. He turned red. Rebecca couldn't tell if he was blushing or angry. He didn't say anything for a long time.

Then he walked into the closet without even looking back at Rebecca. Several kids started to yell. "Way to go, Rebecca!" Samantha glared at her.

Rebecca opened the door to the closet and stepped in, leaving it open just a crack. Inside, it was almost completely dark except for the thin ribbon of light coming from the bottom. Gradually Rebecca's eyes adjusted. Scott was standing with his head practically buried under a coat.

"Scott?" Rebecca asked.

"Yup," said Scott. "I'm here."

Rebecca pushed to the back of the closet with him. She didn't know exactly what to do now.

"We've got seven minutes," said Rebecca.

"Luckily, I've got a watch with a glow-in-the-dark dial," said Scott. He held up his left wrist with his right hand and showed her the watch. Together he and Rebecca watched seven seconds go by. Seven seconds seemed like a very long time. Gradually the second hand made a complete circle.

"One minute gone," said Scott. Rebecca wondered if they really were going to spend the entire seven minutes watching time go by. She was dying to know why Scott had come into the closet with her instead of answering the question.

"Two minutes," Scott declared a minute later.

Rebecca couldn't stand it any longer. She pulled his hand away from his other wrist. "Scott, are we going to spend the entire seven minutes calling out the minutes?"

"What do you want to do?" Scott asked.

"Why did you come in here with me?" Rebecca demanded. She was still holding on to Scott's right hand. "You could have made up some answer," she whispered. "You could have said chocolate—chocolate ice cream, great drum music, and noodles with butter. Those are three of your favorite things. You could have said—'Those things make my life perfect.'"

Rebecca wanted Scott to say, *I didn't answer the question because I wanted to come in here and kiss you. I guess when it comes down to it, you and dancing with you make my life perfect.*

But Scott didn't say those words. "You forgot dancing," he mumbled. "I like dancing." Then he added the words "with you" so low that Rebecca could barely hear them.

He held his left hand up to show Rebecca his watch. "Three minutes," he said. That's when they both realized that Rebecca was still holding his right hand. Scott squeezed her hand. Rebecca turned to face him. A coat landed on her head.

She started to giggle. Scott pulled the coat off of her. He let it fall to the bottom of the closet.

Rebecca moved her head closer to Scott's. They brought their hands up, almost the way they did when they danced. Scott wiggled his toes a few inches closer to Rebecca.

They both moved their heads toward each other again. Their lips were almost touching. Rebecca tilted her head back. Scott brought his left hand up. Rebecca felt his fingers gently touching her along her spine and then on the back of her neck.

Suddenly, Scott gave a little yelp. He jumped back. "Please tell me there's not a dead cat in here," he begged in a whisper.

Rebecca's hands flew to her head. Her wig had come off in Scott's hands. "It's my wig," giggled Rebecca.

"I thought it was an animal," gasped Scott. Suddenly Rebecca and Scott were giggling so hard they couldn't stop.

They heard a knocking on the closet door. "Time's up!" shouted Samantha. Rebecca and Scott fell out of the closet, gasping for air. Scott still had Rebecca's wig in his hand. Every time they tried to stop laughing, they'd look at each other and started up again.

"What's so funny?" Samantha asked, furious.

Scott and Rebecca stopped for a second. Then they began snorting and laughing again.

"Apparently heaven's a very funny place," said Adrienne.

17

Where's Second Base?

Rebecca was in a great mood. She had told her
parents that the Anti-Valentine's Day Monster
Mash had been the best party ever. She had opened
her presents. Scott had given her a CD of swing
dance music. Adrienne had given her a set of butterfly
clips for her hair. Samantha had given her stationery
with hearts on it. Daniel and Shane had chipped in and
bought her an official WNBA basketball shirt. All in
all, Rebecca had a feeling that being thirteen was
going to be way, way better than being twelve.

Unfortunately, she forgot to calculate the speed
that rumors can travel. Scientists can calculate the
speed of light—but nobody can calculate the speed
of a rumor. By Monday, Daniel greeted Rebecca by
shouting, "Hey, Rebecca! Want to play a little baseball?" He snickered.

Rebecca made a face. "It's February, dummy. Why
would I play baseball in February?"

"Oh, I heard you're great at playing second base," said Daniel slyly.

"I'm a catcher when I play baseball," said Rebecca. "But mainly, I'm a basketball player and dancer. You know that."

"I heard you can play baseball in a closet," sneered Daniel. Rebecca didn't know what he was talking about, but she knew it was nasty.

"Oh, Daniel, grow up," said Rebecca disgustedly.

She moved down the hall. Shane stopped her. "Hey, Rebecca, I heard that it was really hot in the closet at your birthday party."

Rebecca made a face at him. She turned to Samantha. "Do you know what's he's talking about?"

"Everybody knows what he's talking about," said Samantha snidely. She slammed her locker shut.

Rebecca went after her. "What do you mean, *everybody*?"

Samantha turned to Rebecca. "You and Scott. In the closet. You let Scott get to second base."

"What!" exclaimed Rebecca. "I don't even know where second base is. I mean, I know where it is on the baseball diamond . . . but not . . . you *know*! Besides playing Seven Minutes in Heaven was your idea, not mine."

"I didn't mean that you should go into the

closet with Scott!" yelled Samantha. "Maybe he was the one who told his friends about what you two really did in the closet."

"Scott wouldn't lie about something like that," said Rebecca.

"Oh, yeah? Well, maybe it's not a lie, then."

"I was there! I know it was a lie. Wherever second base is—neither Scott nor I went there."

"That's not what everybody is saying."

"Who do you believe, everybody—or me?"

"On this subject, I don't know who to believe," said Samantha dramatically. She turned on her heel and walked away. Rebecca ran her hand through her hair and pulled at it hard. When she did, she remembered the moment just before Scott's hand had come up with her wig. Their lips had come so close to touching. She could remember the feel of Scott's hand on her back. Was it possible? Could Scott have lied about what went on? Rebecca didn't believe it.

Rebecca tracked Scott down by the bulletin board about the core virtues outside the principal's office. "We've got to talk," she said.

"Do you know that those are the scariest words in the English language?" said Scott. "Think about it—your parents say, 'We've got to talk.' It either means that you're in trouble or they're getting a divorce. If a teacher says it, you know you're flunking. Tell me one good thing that could possibly happen after somebody says, 'We've got to talk.'"

"You could find out the truth," said Rebecca. "Look, Scott, I said the exact same thing to my mom, but there are times when it's true. We really do have to talk."

Scott seemed to be finding the bulletin board fascinating. There were quotations about every virtue: trustworthiness, kindness, caring, courtesy, hard work, respect, responsibility, self-control, honesty, and fairness.

"You know," said Scott, "maybe Divinas is on to something. We are building a culture of characters. We've got a lot of characters in this school. You're certainly one of them."

"Scott, stop dancing around the subject. We've got to talk about what people are saying about us."

Scott didn't answer. He was leaning against the bulletin board as if he didn't have a care in the world. His left hand happened to fall on trustworthiness. Rebecca was so angry that she took his hand and shoved it off the board. She held on to it tight, remembering the moment she had held on to Scott's hand in the closet. "Haven't you heard what people

117

are saying about us?" she demanded through gritted teeth.

Scott took his hand back. "Yeah, they're saying that we did more than kiss in the closet." He sounded completely unruffled.

Rebecca shoved him in the chest. "You jerk! How can you say that so calmly? You know we didn't do anything!"

"Exactly," said Scott. "You and I know it's a stupid lie. So why should it bother us? What are you getting so worked up about?"

Rebecca blinked. "Why . . . why . . . how can it not bother you? Never mind. Of course, it doesn't bother you. You get to be the big stud that everybody's fighting over. You're loving this."

Scott couldn't seem to stop staring at the bulletin board. "I thought after . . . you know . . ." he stammered.

"You know, what?" Rebecca asked.

"Well, after you and me in the closet—you know."

"But nothing happened, did it?" insisted Rebecca.

"I don't think so," said Scott. "Did you think something happened?"

Rebecca thought about the moment before they had started laughing. It was almost as if they were back in third grade again. Whatever happened, they weren't talking about it. Scott looked at his watch. "We've got dance class in two minutes," he said.

"Do you really think we can keep dancing together now that everyone is talking about us?" Rebecca asked. She wanted to Scott to say, *Of course we have to dance together—because I love dancing with you and we're such a good team.*

But Scott kept messing up the scripts that she wrote for him. "What choice do we have?" he said. "I don't think Mr. DePalma will let us change partners."

"Is that what you want to do?" Rebecca asked. "Change partners?"

"You're the one who's so mad about the rumors. What do you want to do?" Scott walked away without waiting for an answer. Rebecca was left staring at the bulletin board. She blinked back tears as she read the quotes about trust:

It is an equal failing to trust everybody, and to trust nobody.
English proverb (18th century)

It is impossible to go through life without trust: that is to be imprisoned in the worst cell of all, oneself.
Graham Greene, British novelist (1943)

Trust everybody, but cut the cards.
Finley Peter Dunne, U.S. humorist (1900)

18

It's Torture to Just Watch

"**W**ere you fighting with Scott?" Samantha asked.

"It wasn't exactly a fight," said Rebecca. "I'm not sure exactly what it was."

"You know, if you still dance together," said Samantha, "it won't look good. People will just keep spreading rumors about you."

Rebecca sighed, blinking back a tear. She didn't want to quit dancing with Scott, but maybe Samantha was right. Maybe there wasn't a choice. Rebecca went into dance class. She saw Mr. DePalma across the room.

"Hi, Rebecca. Happy birthday!" he said. "I've got the perfect present for you. It's going to be a lot of fun. Now that we've learned the basics of swing, I'm going to start the class doing a few flips. You've probably seen it on television where the girl jumps into the boy's arms and flings her legs in the air. I just know that you and Scott will be great at it."

Rebecca could just imagine what everybody would say if she jumped into Scott's arms and flung her legs around him. "Uh, Mr. DePalma, can I talk to you privately?" Rebecca asked.

"Sure," said Mr. DePalma. He took one look at Rebecca's face. "What's wrong?"

Rebecca paused. Even though this was the wonderful, perfect Mr. DePalma, Rebecca couldn't really imagine telling a teacher about all this stuff.

"See, the thing is, Mr. DePalma. Scott and I, it's gotten a little sticky between us and it might be better . . ." Rebecca realized that she couldn't get out a coherent sentence. She wished she had used any other word but "sticky." Sticky was so—well—gross.

Mr. DePalma held up his hand. "Whoa, Rebecca. Hold it right there. We'll work this out."

Rebecca took her first deep breath all day since she had heard about the rumors. Those were magical words. *We'll work this out*. Mr. DePalma would make it all okay. Maybe he would tell her that he wanted her to take private lessons with him in his studio. After all, he only came to school twice a week. Rebecca would start seeing him every day after school. He would be her partner, not Scott. Rebecca was so deep into her daydream, she almost didn't hear Mr. DePalma call out, "Scott, come over here."

"We don't need him," said Rebecca quickly.

Mr. DePalma looked at her strangely. "Certainly, we do," he said.

Scott came over reluctantly. "Scott, Rebecca tells me there's some problem between the two of you."

Scott looked embarrassed. "Well, it's not exactly a problem," he said.

"The whole school is talking about Scott and me," Rebecca blurted out. "Because Scott kind of goes with Samantha—and, well, Samantha is mad at me . . ."

"I don't understand," said Mr. DePalma. "What does any of this have to do with this class?"

"Because people are saying things about Scott and me," Rebecca whispered miserably. Then she glared at Scott. "And Scott's enjoying it."

"I am not!" said Scott.

"Well, you're not doing anything to stop it," shouted Rebecca.

"What can I do?" asked Scott.

"Something! All you do is stand there and pretend you're so innocent. You had a choice!"

"And you're an emotional yo-yo," shouted Scott. "One minute you're fine and fun, and then you're yelling at me."

"I am not an emotional yo-yo!"

"Scott and Rebecca! Zip it up!" commanded Mr. DePalma.

Scott and Rebecca shut their mouths, but they refused to look at each other. Finally, Rebecca took a deep breath. "Scott and I can't dance together, because people are saying bad stuff about us." Rebecca felt that at least she had boiled it down to a single sentence.

"I won't bend the rules," said Mr. DePalma. "You either dance together or you don't dance at all. I want you to work it out. I told my partner how thrilled I am by the way you two kids connect when you're dancing."

Rebecca was so miserable she didn't even hear the compliment Mr. DePalma was giving them. Everything was falling apart. She loved dancing with Scott and they had a chance to win the trophy, but if they kept dancing, the rumors would never stop.

Mr. DePalma continued. "Why don't you take some time out and think about it? For this class, you can sit on the sidelines and watch if you won't dance. Do you remember, way at the beginning of the year, months ago, when Dr. Divinas talked about your core virtues? I said none of those virtues matters if you don't have a core yourself. You and Scott are going to have to decide if deep in your core you want to dance."

"But if we keep dancing together, everyone will keep talking about us," said Rebecca.

"Well, as the song says, 'Why don't you give them something to talk about' by being the best dancers you can be," said Mr. DePalma. "Now, excuse me, I've got a class to teach."

Rebecca and Scott sat in the bleachers as the class filed in. Mr. DePalma taught the girls how to flip onto the boys' hips by keeping their weight centered and letting their own aerial jump do the work. The boys just had to help their partners keep their balance, not do the actual lifting.

"It's an illusion. It's not how high you go. Remember, less is more."

The whole class laughed because Mr. DePalma said that so often. Each couple stood in front of each other. The girls jumped into the boys' arms. Adrienne looked particularly good, swinging her long legs first to one side of Shane and then jumping back in place and swinging to the left. It all had to be done in tempo. Adrienne and Shane looked like they were having a blast. And it was definitely not fun to have to just sit and watch. In fact, it was torture.

No More Kisses

After school Scott came over to Rebecca's house. He walked into the living room and sat down on the couch next to her. "We need to talk," he said.

Rebecca looked at him. "I thought you said that nothing good could ever come after those words."

"I was wrong. I was wrong about a lot of stuff. I hated sitting while everybody else was dancing. And I hate it when you're mad at me."

"Me, too. Maybe it's my fault. Maybe I should never have played Seven Minutes in Heaven with you."

"I kind of had fun, didn't you?" asked Scott.

"Yeah, but what about Samantha?" said Rebecca.

"See. That's the thing," said Scott. "I've been thinking. This whole kissing thing is the source of the problem."

"Huh?" said Rebecca. This wasn't exactly what she had expected to hear.

"It came to me," said Scott "that kissing is what went wrong. When I kissed Samantha, she started to tell everybody that we were boyfriend and girlfriend. But you didn't seem to care . . ."

"I cared," said Rebecca.

"Well, you never said anything," complained Scott.

"You didn't, either," Rebecca pointed out.

"Okay, anyhow, I took care of Samantha. I told her no more kisses. I think that's a good rule. She doesn't want me to be her boyfriend anymore."

"Oh," said Rebecca. It took all her restraint not to add "good."

"So," continued Scott, "I figured that would be a good rule for us, too. Then we'd be out of trouble."

"No more kisses," repeated Rebecca.

"Yeah, and that way we can dance together," said Scott. "Isn't that a good solution?"

Rebecca wasn't so sure. She remembered reading an article, "Boys Are from Pluto." The article said that boys always liked to come up with solutions, even if it meant that nothing much got better.

"So, we agree. We'll keep dancing together—and forget about that other stuff," confirmed Scott, rising off the couch as if he couldn't wait to get out of there.

"Forget about the kissing stuff," repeated Rebecca

hesitantly, wanting to make sure she understood. They had hardly even gotten to the kissing stuff and now they were swearing it off.

"Yeah," said Scott, refusing to look at her. "But we'll still dance together. We won't quit."

Rebecca nodded. "I like the dancing part," admitted Rebecca. She just wasn't completely sure she wanted to give up the kissing part.

"Good." Scott grinned. "Then it's settled. Phew! I've got to go. See you later," he said quickly and left.

Rebecca blinked. She looked at her watch. He had been there less than seven minutes. They were going backward. Fifteen minutes for a date in third grade. Seven minutes in the closet. Six minutes on the couch. Soon they'd be down to zero. Zero kisses, but they would dance. Rebecca guessed it was a good trade-off. She just wondered why she didn't feel better. Well, for one thing, they really hadn't done anything about the rumors. And for another, Rebecca was a little bit afraid to face Samantha and tell her that she wasn't going to quit dancing with Scott.

When Rebecca's father came home from work, he found her in the exact same position that Scott had left her in, sitting on the living room couch, staring into space. Rebecca hadn't even bothered to turn on the lights or the TV.

Her father came in and turned on the lights. "Rebecca, I didn't even realize that you were here. Are you hiding in the dark for some reason?"

"Yes," said Rebecca. "It reminds me of the closet." She sighed. "I kind of liked it in the closet."

Her father came and sat beside her. "What?"

"Nothing," sighed Rebecca, already afraid that she had said too much.

"What's bothering you?" her father asked.

"Well, people are kind of saying some stuff about me and Scott, and Samantha says that the rumors would stop if I quit dancing with him, but Scott and I don't want to."

"What kind of stuff?" asked her father suspiciously.

"Just stuff," said Rebecca vaguely. "But it's not true."

"Then I don't see why you and Scott should stop doing something you love."

"What about Samantha and the rumors? I know Samantha thinks we should quit," said Rebecca.

"Would a real friend want to hold you back? It's obvious that you and Scott have not only been friends forever but also love to dance together. Why doesn't Samantha believe you? Why did she believe the rumors and not you?"

"I don't know," said Rebecca.

"Well, maybe you should find out," said her father.

Rebecca swallowed. Finding out would be scary.

The next morning, Rebecca vowed to herself that she wouldn't go through another wimpy day. Not one more wimpy day in which she would feel the way she had felt yesterday when she had sat in the bleachers and watched everybody else dance.

Rebecca glanced down the hall. She saw Samantha standing by her locker, joking with a bunch of kids.

"Hey," said Rebecca. "There's something I've got to ask you."

"Shoot," said Samantha breezily.

"Why didn't you believe me when I told you that Scott and I didn't do anything?"

Samantha stared at Rebecca. "Well . . . I . . . everyone was talking . . . and you and Scott were giggling when you came out of the closet."

"We were giggling because my wig came off," said Rebecca. "Not because we had done anything."

"Well, still," said Samantha. "There were all those rumors, and if you and Scott keep dancing together, the rumors won't stop."

"Can you think of any stupider reason for me to quit dancing?" asked Rebecca. "To quit because of some stupid rumors that aren't even true?"

"It would be so much easier for you to quit," insisted Samantha.

"Easier for who?" said Rebecca. "Maybe for you. You're probably the one who started the rumors. You never even wanted Scott as a boyfriend until he and I started dancing together. It was the one thing in the world that I could do better than you."

Samantha refused to look at Rebecca. "You're not being very nice," she said. "I think Scott is a child. I'm going to get back together with Shane. Did you know Scott wants to have a 'no kissing' rule? He's such a baby."

"I can live with it. You know, way back, you said Scott shouldn't be my boyfriend because he and I knew each other too well. You said I shouldn't have a boyfriend who's a friend. But you were wrong. Scott's my best friend."

"You can't have a boyfriend as your best friend," said Samantha scornfully. "It's unnatural."

"Just watch us," said Rebecca. "Even with no kisses. I feel sorry for Shane." Rebecca walked past the bulletin board on core virtues. It was funny. There were a lot of virtues up there—hard work, respect, self-control. Mr. DePalma had hit the nail on the head. None of those virtues mattered if you didn't have a core. Dancers danced from their core. Rebecca felt hers. It felt solid. It felt good.

You Can't Fake Passion

The no kisses rule worked—at least on the surface. People stopped talking about them. Scott and Rebecca continued to dance. Life was back to a normal. A little bit boring, but normal.

Rebecca and Scott's dancing kept getting better. Although they practiced the tango and merengue, they both felt that swing was their best dance. They quickly picked up the flips that Mr. DePalma had taught. They got really good at what Mr. DePalma called the West Coast swing that had started in California. It had an eight-count beat and it was danced very fast like the Charleston. The partners danced side by side, not facing each other, hardly touching. Rebecca and Scott had gotten so they could dance it even when the music got so fast that the other dancers lost it.

At the end of April, Mr. DePalma gathered everybody around him. "Girls and boys, it's time for me to announce the couples that will be representing our school at the citywide competition next week. You've all worked hard, but we can only enter one couple per dance. However, I expect all of you to come to the championships and cheer our school on. I've chosen two couples from this group and the rest from the other classes that I work with from this school."

Rebecca and Scott looked at each other. They were so quick on their feet, they felt sure that they would be picked. Everyone knew they were the best at swing.

"The couple representing the William T. Harris school doing swing will be Adrienne and Shane," announced Mr. DePalma. Rebecca and Scott tried not to make a face, but they were both very disappointed. Mr. DePalma announced the winners for the fox-trot and the merengue, who were not from their group. Each time their names were not announced, Rebecca felt worse. She couldn't believe it. She had thought they were so good. Was this really happening? Were they not going to be picked at all?

"And the couple representing you in the tango will be Scott and Rebecca," said Mr. DePalma.

Scott and Rebecca stared at each other. "We're no good at tango," whispered Scott to Rebecca. "It's our worst dance."

"We've gotta talk to him," said Rebecca. "Maybe he made a mistake."

Scott and Rebecca went up to Mr. DePalma. "Uh, Mr. DePalma, I don't think tango is the best dance for Rebecca and me," said Scott.

"Yeah," said Rebecca. "We aren't so good at those close dances. We're really good at swing, though, don't you think?"

Mr. DePalma looked at them. "You are good at swing. But I picked you for the tango for a reason."

Rebecca ignored him. "See, we haven't practiced the tango as much as swing."

"Rebecca, I've made up my mind. It's very hard for kids—or anyone for that manner—to dance the tango and not look silly. You have to be good and you have to be serious and you have to be able to dance close. The closeness is what makes the tango so unique. I picked you because I believe there is something special about the way you and Scott dance together. A lot will be riding on your dance. Dancing tango is a lot like playing the cleanup hitter in baseball. Competitions are often won or lost by the tango team because it's such a challenging and romantic dance."

When Mr. DePalma said the words "romantic," Rebecca and Scott couldn't look at each other. Mr.

DePalma put a hand on each of their shoulders. "I wouldn't have picked you if I didn't have confidence in you. I've been noticing that there's been less passion in your dancing lately. You've been practicing hard, but something's missing. That's why I decided to give you a challenge."

"Are you sure the challenge couldn't be something else except the tango?" asked Scott.

"Come on, you two. You know the steps perfectly. You've got a wonderful precision. All you need is just that little extra something. Let me see it. Take your positions."

Scott put his right hand around Rebecca's back. Rebecca put her right hand up, and Scott took it.

"Closer," insisted Mr. DePalma. "No other dance connects two people more closely than the tango. You have to be emotionally as well as physically in sync. You must keep your arms around each other for the entire dance. I want you to think of yourselves as two jungle cats moving as one."

"Now we're supposed to be eight feet pretending to be two," Rebecca joked. Scott giggled.

"Cut out the laughing, you two," said Mr. DePalma. "Hold up your heads, and concentrate on the dance—don't let anything interfere with that."

Mr. DePalma put on the music. Scott and

Rebecca fit their bodies into each other, keeping their upper bodies close the way they had been taught. They slowly moved around the circle, counting out the rhythm of the steps.

"That's good," said Mr. DePalma. "But, connect! Connect!"

Scott sandwiched his left foot in between Rebecca's leg. Rebecca whipped her right foot around his, snapping her head to the left the way Mr. DePalma had taught them.

"Excellent, excellent," said Mr. DePalma. "I knew I picked the right couple. Now, just bring me more passion! I know you're kids, but you can dance it with feeling. Don't just get the steps right. You have to listen to each other. Bring that to your dance."

Rebecca and Scott took up their positions again. This time when Rebecca did her head fling, she tossed her head dramatically, as if she were an actress.

"No, no," said Mr. DePalma. "Rebecca, you can't fake passion. It comes from inside you."

"Your core," said Rebecca, feeling chastened. "Your center."

"Yes," said Mr. DePalma. "Don't worry. It will come."

Rebecca was glad that Mr. DePalma had faith, but

she wished she understood how to find her core when she needed it. Rebecca and Scott practiced until they had sweat rolling down their backs. They weren't perfect, but they didn't give up. They were dancing the tango.

21

Going Forward by Going Backward

he day after Rebecca and Scott were chosen as finalists, Samantha called. "I'm having a party next Friday night. Maybe you can come after school this week and help me with the decorations. It will be great. I'm so glad I broke up with Scott. Now I can invite tons of interesting boys to my party on Friday night."

"That's the night before the contest," stammered Rebecca. "That's not a good night for a party. It will be terrible for Adrienne and Shane, too. I thought you were back together with Shane."

"We've always been nonexclusive, and there's this new boy, Jonathan, who's adorable."

"I think it's a terrible night for a party," said Rebecca again.

"It's too late to change. I've already told tons of people. So will you come over after school and help me tomorrow?"

"Scott and I are practicing every day after school until the contest."

"Well, I'm not inviting Scott. It would be creepy to have my ex-boyfriend there." Rebecca rolled her eyes as she listened to Samantha.

"Samantha, I don't want to go to a party if Scott can't come," Rebecca said evenly.

"We're going to play Seven Minutes in Heaven and you'll miss out." It was as if Samantha hadn't even heard her.

"Samantha," repeated Rebecca, losing patience. "I can't come to your party if Scott isn't invited. Besides, I told you, it's the night before the contest. Mr. DePalma told us that we should get some rest."

"You really think the stupid dance contest is more important than my party?"

"It's not some stupid dance contest!" Rebecca was really getting mad. "And if Scott can't come, I won't, either."

"But Scott isn't your boyfriend."

"He's my partner and my friend," said Rebecca, and she hung up the phone. She had never really thought about it, but that's exactly what Scott was— her partner and her friend.

The day before the contest, Scott and Rebecca were practicing when Scott casually asked, "Are you going to Samantha's party?"

Rebecca shook her head. "Naw, I told her that both you and I had to practice."

"Nice try. She already told me that she was having a party and not inviting me," said Scott. "Samantha's a piece of work. I wouldn't want to go to her party even if she did invite me."

"Are you mad at her because she broke up with you?" asked Rebecca.

"Well actually, it was kind of the other way around," said Scott. "I broke up with her. I didn't like the way she was talking about you. You're my partner. She called you a boyfriend stealer. I know you didn't do anything. I told her I didn't want to be her boyfriend anymore."

Rebecca smiled at him. "I told her that I wouldn't go because she wouldn't invite you. But Samantha says that she was the one who broke up with you."

"Why does any of this even matter?" Scott demanded. "Can we please stop talking about it? We've got a chance to win the dance contest—and all the other stuff just gets in the way."

"I really want to win."

"Well, so do I," admitted Scott. "It would be awful to be with a partner who didn't want to win."

Rebecca and Scott practiced their tango moves.

They had to dance extremely close in order to do it correctly. "I hear they're going to play Seven Minutes in Heaven all night at Samantha's party," said Scott out of the blue into Rebecca's ear.

"Do you wish you could go?" Rebecca asked.

Scott moved Rebecca into a quick turn to the left. "No. I think it's a stupid game."

"Me, too." Rebecca agreed quickly. She gave Scott a sideways glance as she did her head flick. She kept wondering what it would be like to really kiss Scott, but maybe not for seven minutes.

On the morning of the contest Rebecca glanced across the room at the photo of her great-grand-mother in the Model T. Rebecca picked up the photo just as the phone rang. It was Samantha.

"How was your party?" asked Rebecca.

"It was fabulous," said Samantha. She giggled. "We played Seven Minutes in Heaven for hours—it was so much fun. You should have come. I kissed that boy Jonathan. He's a much better kisser than Scott or Shane."

"I bet he's not a better dancer," Rebecca muttered.

"What?" asked Samantha.

"Nothing. I've got to go."

When her mother came into the room she saw

Rebecca hugging the picture of her great-grand-mother. "Did you ever meet her?" Rebecca asked as she put down the photo.

"Yes," said her mother. "She danced at our wedding. Your father and she danced so beautifully together that even though she was eighty-nine, I was jealous. She would have been proud of you today. Let me help you get dressed."

Rebecca's mother helped her put on the white dress with the lavender ribbon. She did Rebecca's hair. Then she stepped back and looked at Rebecca proudly in the mirror. "Go show your father," she said.

Rebecca went downstairs. "You look beautiful," said her father, "especially without the gray wig. You look like a lovely young lady, not a grandmother."

"We were just talking about your grandmother, the original Rebecca," said Rebecca's mother.

"Our Rebecca's pretty original, too," said her father. "You know, Rebecca, in that dress I bet you look like the original Rebecca when she was a girl. I think you act like her, too. You don't go backward through life."

"That's not true. When I do the tango with Scott, I have to go backward," Rebecca said. "And you always told me that my namesake hated going backward."

"I think deep down she understood that some-times you have to go backward to go forward," said her father. Rebecca realized it would have been going backward to go to Samantha's kissing party without Scott. If she had listened to Samantha, she and Scott would never be going to the dance contest.

"That's kind of like when Mr. DePalma gets all mystical and talks about our core," said Rebecca.

"Well, I know that's the highest compliment I could get," said her father, laughing. "You learned a lot from him this year. I'm glad he's your teacher."

"And he's so cute," said her mother.

Rebecca rolled her eyes. She still didn't like her mother calling Mr. DePalma cute.

22

Dance from Your Core and Let Your Centers Find Each Other

Rebecca's parents drove her to the dance contest. They had to be there an hour before it began. It was held in a hotel ballroom. There were potted palm trees all around the dance floor with ribbons for the competing school flowing from the palm leaves. The color for the William T. Harris School was yellow. Rebecca looked around for Scott. She couldn't find him. Adrienne and Shane were there. Even Shane looked petrified. He could hardly speak.

There were television cameras being set up. "Where's Scott?" asked Rebecca nervously.

"He'll be here," said Mr. DePalma. Just at that moment, Scott came rushing in with his parents. He was wearing black pants, a white shirt, and a tie with lavender flowers on it.

"Nice tie," said Mr. DePalma.

"We were almost late because he couldn't make up his mind. He picked it out himself," said Mrs.

Lee. She gave Rebecca a hug. "Sweetie, you look so cute."

Mr. DePalma turned to all the parents. "Why don't you all take your seats," he said. "This way you can get some down in the front. And I want to talk to the kids alone."

Mr. DePalma put a sash around each of the girls and pinned numbers on the backs of the boys' shirts. He looked at Scott's number as he pinned it on. "You and Rebecca are couple number seven," he said. "Seven is a lucky number."

Mr. DePalma gathered the couples from the William T. Harris School around him. "I know you're all feeling nervous. That's natural. The adrenaline will work for you. But take a moment before you start to dance to breathe. Don't move right away. Take the time at the beginning to connect with your partners. Just remember. Dance from your core—and let your centers find each other."

They were all too scared to talk. Mr. DePalma went off to discuss some last-minute arrangements with the master of ceremonies. Rebecca checked to see if Scott's number was straight. Scott turned around to face her. "You look pretty in that dress."

"Do you miss the Bride of Frankenstein wig?" Rebecca asked him.

"No," said Scott. "It always reminded me of a dead cat . . . even outside of the closet."

"Are you nervous?" asked Rebecca.

"I feel like I may throw up," said Scott.

Rebecca looked at him. "Please don't," she begged.

"I'll try not to," he replied.

Mr. DePalma came back. "We're about to begin. "They want you all to march in by couples. It will be a promenade. Get ready." Scott offered Rebecca's his arm. She rested her hand lightly on his forearm.

Samantha came rushing up to them. "Good luck." Then she snidely added, "Rebecca, I hope you don't step on Scott's toe."

"Samantha, get over yourself," said Rebecca. Scott and Rebecca turned their backs on her and promenaded toward the stage.

"Are you okay?" asked Scott.

"Yeah. She makes me so mad, though!" said Rebecca.

"Good." Scott smiled. "You dance the tango better when you're angry."

The lights were bright on the dance floor. They promenaded in front of the audience. Rebecca thought she could hear her father's loud cheers as she and Scott walked by. Then they watched the other couples dance the merengue and the fox-trot. The crowd was loving it. There were *oohs* and *ahhs*, and cheers from the different schools. The judges stalked around the dance floor, taking notes in front of each couple. Rebecca, Scott, Adrienne, and Shane had a long time to wait and watch, and the waiting was nerve-racking.

Finally it was Adrienne and Shane's turn with swing. "Good luck," Rebecca whispered to them both.

"I think I'm going to throw up," whispered Shane.

"Just try not to do it on Adrienne," Rebecca advised him. "That's what I told Scott." She patted Shane on the back. "You'll be great."

Shane sighed. He bowed his head. He really did look like he was going to throw up. Yet when he and Adrienne took the stage, something electrified them both. They grinned at the audience. Shane got down real low, as he led Adrienne in. He looked cool and snazzy. He snapped his fingers. Then he swung Adrienne out, and she jumped back into his arm, swinging her legs out over his hips. They did their shimmy, and the audience burst into applause. When they finished their dance they were both breathing hard.

"You were fantastic!" exclaimed Rebecca. Shane still looked as if he might throw up. Adrienne and Shane held each other's hands as they waited for the judges' decision. They screamed when they came in third. Rebecca and Scott gave them each a high five, then looked at each other. They still had their own dance to do.

23

Sometimes, Seven Seconds Can Seem Like Heaven

At last it was time for the tango, the final dance of the competition. Rebecca and Scott took the stage with the other ten competing couples doing the tango from other schools.

Mr. DePalma adjusted their arms so that they were in the right position. Rebecca's cheek was next to Scott's, their toes touching. "Remember, you start out going backward on your right foot," Scott whispered.

"I remember," said Rebecca, annoyed. That had been their first lesson. She didn't need him to treat her like an idiot. She held her head up high.

The music started. Scott held her close. They both took a deep breath at the same moment. Their lungs filled with air and then they let it out slowly. They looked into each other's eyes for a moment. The anger disappeared. They listened to the music. Then they turned their heads away from each other, but moved closer so their upper bodies were touching. At the slight pressure from Scott's touch, Rebecca took a backward step directly on the beat.

They went into their tango box step, Scott mouthing the words, "Slow, quick quick, slow, quick quick." Then they did a quick head snap and made a perfect scorpion tail above their heads. They moved into the rock step. They rocked gently back and forth, not taking big steps, but every step they took was precise.

The other couples were moving around the dance floor with more speed and more drama, but Rebecca and Scott stayed within themselves. They hadn't made a mistake yet. Rebecca hooked her leg around Scott, Scott forgot her leg was there and started to trip. Rebecca held her back straight and kept her balance long enough for Scott to recover gracefully.

Scott boldly led Rebecca into her backward pause. They kept their weight on the balls of their feet, like two jungle cats, and they both pulled toward each other and pushed away. They could feel exactly what the other was doing. They moved around the line of dance in a countercircle, filling the space. The music moved them. Their bodies were pulsing together to the beat. They were tense

150

dancing in front of an audience, but it was also a rush. When it was over, Rebecca looked over her left shoulder, her toe and leg in a perfect extension.

Then they broke apart, blinking into the lights.

"You were fantastic!" whispered Mr. DePalma as he came up to them. "Now we wait."

The judges seemed to take forever to make their decisions. "Everybody is a winner today," said the judge. "First, I'd like to call up the couple from the Hamilton School to come get their medal for the tango."

Rebecca watched as school after school and couple after couple were called to get their medals. They were so wound-up that at first they didn't realize that the couples being announced were the runners-up. "We lost," moaned Rebecca slinking behind one of the potted palms. Then it was down to two couples. That's when it dawned on them. They were either going to come in first or second. Scott took Rebecca's hand.

"And now, ladies and gentleman, boys and girls. The first runners-up in the tango are the couple from Austin Avenue School. And let's hear it for our champion tango dance team, Rebecca Luzzaro and Scott Lee from William T. Harris School!"

Rebecca jumped into the air and hugged Scott. They kept jumping up and down until their heads

smacked together with a *crack*! It was so loud that even Mr. DePalma winced.

"Ouch!" said Scott, rubbing his forehead. Rebecca rubbed hers.

"You're both killer dancers," said Mr. DePalma. "As I told you before, I consider that a great compliment. Now go on, you have to get the trophy."

Scott and Rebecca went up to the judges. They waved the trophy over their heads. Scott's and Rebecca's parents came up and hugged them. Adrienne and Shane gave them both high fives.

The TV crews put their cameras away. The ballroom lights dimmed. Rebecca and Scott and their families were among the last to leave. Rebecca and Scott went to get their jackets. The check person had already gone and the coat closet appeared to be empty except for Rebecca's and Scott's jackets. Rebecca's jacket hung way in the back.

She made her way through the jungle of hangers. Scott was right behind her. Rebecca got her jacket and turned, bumping into Scott. They stood toe to toe the way they did when they danced, and neither backed away.

"I loved winning." Rebecca was flushed with excitement.

"Me, too," Scott murmured.

They stood against the back of the closet, smiling at each other.

Scott couldn't quite look at her. Finally he said hesitantly, "About my no kissing rule . . ."

"I was going to ask you about it," whispered Rebecca. "How long do we have to live with it?"

"Maybe it's not a good rule." Scott was leaning in closer.

This time they weren't in third grade. There was no wig on Rebecca's head. And it wasn't a game. This wasn't about anybody else. It was just about them. Their lips touched and they didn't push each other away. Scott's lips were softer than Rebecca remembered. Rebecca put her arms around Scott's neck. She could feel his arms around her waist. She felt warm and safe and excited. Safe and excited—it was weird that such different sensations could go together—but they did.

When they finally broke apart, they stood awkwardly. Rebecca looked at Scott, thinking how easy it was to read his face. He looked happy, and excited, too. Scott grinned at her. He looked at his watch. "I think that lasted seven seconds," he said.

Rebecca laughed. "Sometimes, seven seconds can seem like heaven."

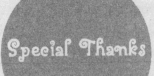
Special Thanks

To Pierre Dulaine from the American Ballroom Theater for his inspiration and his wonderful way with children, and to Pam Greenspan for letting me watch her great ballroom dancing classes with children. To Emilyn Garrick, teacher and friend, whose good spirit, fun, and love of her students made we want to dance up those long flights of stairs to her room at P.S. 11. To all the authors of Class 5-404 in New York City who shared their stories of dancing from the heart with me in 1998–9. To Paula Danziger, who kept me focused and laughing and never let me quit trying to make the book stronger and more real. To Robie Harris, who believed in this book from the beginning. To Dr. Murray List, who wants both my characters and me to dance at the highest level. And finally, to two extraordinary editors at Hyperion who made this book so much better, Alessandra Balzer and Erin McCormack.